RING OF THORNS

A Unit 1 novel – Book 6

ALLEN KENT

AllenPearce Publishers © ▭ ©

Library of Congress Cataloging-in-Publication Data
Allen Kent
Ring of Thorns
Kent, Allen
Cover Design: Jillian Farnsworth
ISBN: 978-1-7332173-8-5

Allen Kent © 2020

To Holly:
My Love and Partner in Adventure

ACKNOWLEDGMENTS

Grateful thanks to my team of readers: my wife Holly, Diane Andris, Marilyn Jenson, Alison Koralewski, Judy Day, Juliet Scherer, and Richard Clement.
You all made this a much better book.
And special thanks to Jillian Farnsworth for her wonderful cover!

SOUTHERN AFRICA

1

The pilot leaned suddenly forward against his harness, muttering a silent oath and staring intently at the instrument panel. If his face showed alarm, it remained hidden behind a pair of dark aviator glasses and a tangle of russet beard. He tapped aggressively at one of the smaller gauges.

"We need to find a place to put this thing down," he muttered to the woman who sat beside him in the copilot's seat, a white-knuckled grip on its padded arms. Though his voice remained calm, the message pulled her sharply forward. She made no effort to hide the panic that swept across her colorless face.

"Oh, my God! What's wrong?"

"We're losing torque. And the oil pressure's dropping. I need to put her down before the engine seizes."

The woman had thrown up violently over an hour ago, losing what little she had in her stomach to the constant jarring of wings that bounced and swayed through super-heated air. She glanced frantically out the window to her right. "There's nothing down there but open bush country," she whimpered, then lurched hard against her own harness with gut-wrenching dry heaves.

The pilot throttled back and began a gradual descending turn, studying the dry, barren landscape that stretched without interruption to every horizon. In an effort to maximize fuel economy and stay below flight-tracking radar, he had kept the single-engine Kodiak at 7000 feet since passing Zambezi and entering Angolan airspace. That placed the light commuter aircraft only 1000 feet above the ragged plain, and the turbocharged engine was quickly losing its grip on the sweltering tropical air.

He glanced quickly over at the woman who swallowed a sour

belch and clutched desperately at her stomach. Gradually he eased the plane back to the right toward a bare stretch of sand that bordered a meandering river.

"Pressure's dropping fast," he said as calmly as the constriction in his throat and chest allowed. "Are you strapped in tight?"

She groped frantically at her harness, sucked in a wheezing breath, and threw herself back hard against the seat. "Oh, God! *We're going to die.*" Her voice was a shrill whimper.

"I think I can put her down on her wheels," he murmured. "But the sand may be soft and pitch us forward. Get your arms up in front of your face and brace yourself."

"Oh, Matt . . ." she sobbed, casting a final frantic look at the lifeless expanse of thorny brush that rushed toward them before throwing her elbows up and cupping her hands behind her head. She felt the plane bank left, level momentarily, then the nose pull slightly upward. The Kodiak's rear landing gear slammed into the baked mud of the riverbed, the low-slung fuselage scraping against something that threatened to rip its belly open. The plane ricocheted momentarily back into the air, then settled hard again onto its tires. She heard Matt jam the throttle back against its stop and ventured a peek between clamped elbows. The plane veered left toward the opening of a narrow wash, no wider than the craft's wingspan, lurching forward through heavy gravel and shuddering to a halt, wings straddling the low clay walls of the gully. The propeller stuttered through a final reluctant rotation. Then there was silence.

Matt Hylton collapsed back into his seat, closed his eyes, and drew a slow, calming breath. Taylor sat for a long moment frozen in place, then let her arms drop into her lap and burst into tears.

"I thought we were going to die," she choked between sobs. "What happened? There was no good place to land."

Matt slowly opened his eyes and, without looking over, reached for her arm. "Are you okay, Taylor?"

"Okay?" she sobbed. "We've just crashed! What went wrong?"

He released her arm and tapped again at one of the gauges. "I'm not sure. The oil pressure just dropped to nothing. Broken line? Oil pump? It's hard to screw up one of these engines, but they've done such a piss-poor job of maintaining this one." He turned to his seatmate and again placed a reassuring hand on her arm. "But we're safely down, and the old girl didn't break apart."

She wiped her nose against the back of her hand, then threw her head back to gulp in settling breaths. They sat in silence, letting heartrates return to normal as they gazed about at the scrubby brush that lined both sides of the narrow ravine.

"Where do you think we are?" she murmured finally.

He gave her arm a reassuring squeeze, then rescued the chart from the floor that had been spread across his knee when they began their unexpected descent. He tapped at one edge, then traced a finger across its center. "If this was going to happen, we couldn't have picked a worse place—or better. We're about a hundred miles into Angola, somewhere midway between Zambezi and Kuito. This is probably the most desolate spot in the country."

She tilted forward and looked again at the tangle of thorny brush a few inches from their wingtip.

"What can be good about that?" she wondered, the sob returning to her throat.

He sniffed cynically. "It's the perfect place to crash if you don't want to be found."

2

"Nicholas Page?" Dreu asked. "Isn't that your old flying buddy?" She was seated before a bank of screens, keyboards, and monitors in the second-floor nerve center of Unit 1's Scottsdale condominium, scanning through secure communiques that circulated among offices two thousand miles away at CIA headquarters in Langley, Virginia. The electronic equipment surrounding her covered an island that filled the center of the open room. Its interconnected cyber-brain showcased the latest in artificial intelligence and under the artful guidance of its brilliant mistress, tirelessly synthesized the world's media outlets and probed its most secure intelligence networks, ready to find and feed her any morsel of information she requested.

Adam Zak turned from a projected map of Afghanistan that filled one of the center's walls. His morning had been spent nervously monitoring the progress of Manny Beg as their agent made his way by horseback through the treacherous Badghis region that bordered Turkmenistan, carrying a list of Taliban informants working within the Afghan government.

"There must be a hundred Nick Pages," he said casually, his face reflecting greater concern than his tone suggested. "What are they saying about this one?"

Dreu Sason turned back to her closest screen. "This one is a pilot, like your friend. And has had some connection to the Agency. I thought that might be more than coincidence. He's missing. And the Langley people are looking for him."

Adam was on his feet and moving toward her with a speed that startled the striking, raven-haired woman at the console. "Missing where? What does it say about him?"

"It's been a little complicated to follow," she said, sliding to one side to allow him to pull a rolling chair up beside her. "The first exchange was a message to the Director of Operations from someone in the Clandestine Activities Division. It simply said, "We believe we have located Nicholas Page. Now going by Matthew Hylton. Location: Kabwe, Zambia."

Adam scanned the screens in front of them. "Anything else?"

"A brief reply that said, 'Send details.' Then this." She pointed at a letter-sized document on one of the side monitors, a three-paragraph memo with photo.

To: DO
From: CA Africa Desk

Two American citizens reported missing in Zambia. Both part of an anthropological dig in the Broken Hill Mine area of the city of Kabwe.

Female: Taylor Dennis. 30. Masters in Anthropology, Brown University. Assistant Team Leader. Hometown – Oxford, MS

Male: Matthew Hylton. 38. Team pilot. Claims to be former USAF. Reported prior flying experience with regional European airlines. Home – West Covina, CA. Man in photo below identified internally through facial recognition as Nicholas Page.

Adam leaned into the photograph of ten men and women lined up beside a Daher Kodiak 100 aircraft. Eight were dressed as he would expect anthropologists working in Africa to dress: khaki shorts, assorted T-shirts, bandanas, ankle-high boots. The exceptions were a thin, long-faced man with a short, professorial beard who looked to be in his sixties, and a younger man with a mustache that bent around the corners of his mouth, wearing a canvas safari hat. Both men wore long-sleeved khaki shirts and full-length trousers. Though the mustache was a change and the brim of the hat covered the younger man's forehead to his brow, Adam recognized the deeply scarred face and lop-sided grin of Nick Page.

Dreu leaned back in her chair and watched her partner curiously. "Is that your friend?"

Adam replied with a grunting nod, scanning the line of faces. "Any idea who this Taylor Dennis is?"

"This photo is from the *Times of Zambia*, the leading English-speaking newspaper in the country. It's a few months old. I'm searching for the article but, ironically, it's harder to get than internal Agency memos."

Adam sniffed absently, his eyes still studying the photograph. "I'd guess this one," he ventured, pointing to the woman with short blond hair who stood beside Page. She barely came to his shoulder, was trim and tanned, with what Adam guessed to be light eyes and a pretty, but serious, face. "She looks the most American of the six women—and she's making a point of being close to him."

Dreu grinned over at him. "The most American? Could you have picked *me* out of a photo on that basis?" Dreu's parents, an Indian beauty from Mumbai and a Spanish physicist from Malaga, had met at Stanford where they had been recruited as guest professors and chosen to stay and marry. The result was a willowy, ebony-haired beauty with dark eyes and a satiny, nut-brown complexion who was often mistaken as Latina.

He shrugged. "You're not from Oxford, Mississippi. This woman looks like she is."

"I'll see what I can find," she said. "But why is the Agency interested in your friend?"

Since Adam and Dreu had taken over control of Unit 1 following the death of Bud Liljigren, who had created the deep-cover group of maverick agents in the early 1960s, they had allowed themselves and their small team of agents one link to their past: a friend who could not be family, could never know what the agent or the Unit did, but was trusted enough that, should it become known, would take the secret to the grave. Dreu's link was Brio, a statuesque black woman she had worked with in New York's fashion industry before dedicating herself to the complex and mysterious world of cybersecurity. Brio's humble roots in the pine forests of rural South Carolina had so infused her with natural humility and appreciation for the gifts her striking face and body provided that Dreu found her a refreshing and lasting friend. Brio had no last name, joking that her mother wasn't certain who had fathered her and didn't want to assign credit to the wrong sonofabitch. Adam's single outside connection to his past was Nicholas Page.

Dreu watched concern cloud her partner's face and steepled her long fingers beneath her chin. "Maybe it's time you told me a little more about Mr. Page," she suggested. "You look like you think he may need our help."

Adam's frown tightened. He sucked in a breath, slumped back in the swivel chair, and focused again on the man in the picture.

"When I was in the Air Force and the crane came through my canopy, killing the student pilot I was flying with and taking my eye, I can't begin to describe the pain—and how stunned and disoriented I was." He turned to look at her more directly, one of those rare moments when she became consciously aware of the slight difference in movement of his prosthetic left eye.

"Every bit of my training told me I should punch out," he continued soberly. "But I was too confused to even do that. In the T-38 we were flying, the instructor sits behind the student, elevated enough to see over the front seat. But the air was screaming through the shattered canopy, blood was all over my face, and I felt like a dagger had been thrust into the center of my brain. I'll be honest, Dreu. I didn't have any idea what to do." His face flushed and his right eye teared at the corners as the memory swept again through him. He drew another long breath and released it slowly.

"And then, there was a voice in my headphones. *Tom, this is Page.*'" Adam grinned darkly at Dreu. "Two names from our past. I was Tom Mercomes then. He was Nick Page." He shook his head slightly, refocusing on the memory.

"Well, here came this voice. *'Tom, this is Page. I'm off your right wing. Do you still have control?'* It was like he inserted himself into my head and cut through all the pain and confusion. I tested the flight controls and everything responded. *'Okay,'* he said. *'Follow me in and I'll talk you to the runway.'* For the next ten minutes, with what little I could see out of my good eye, I just kept him off my wing. He called out the power settings. Told me when to drop the gear and lower flaps. Even when to flare as we approached the ground. I was too badly injured to fly the plane and couldn't even unstrap myself when we got it stopped. When you and I first started to work together and you were poking around in my past, you saw how I was the big Air Force flying hero for landing a plane with a shattered canopy instead of bailing out and letting it dive into the desert with the student's body." The flush deepened and he turned away.

"There was nothing heroic about it, Dreu," he murmured. "It was all Nick Page."

They sat in silence, Adam gnawing at the inside of his cheek, Dreu studying a face that she had rarely seen show such vulnerability. She wanted to take one of the hands that rested on the arm of his chair, but knew he didn't want her sympathy. She waited until he looked up with a wan smile.

"There you have it," he said. "That's why Nick—now Matt Hylton, it seems—and I are so close. In our rare messages, I go by Cyclops. I call him Wingman. He's something of an odd duck. I've wondered sometimes if he has a mild form of Asperger's. Not many social skills but as trustworthy as the day is long."

She pulled him to her, kissed both eyelids and lightly moved to his lips, then smiled and tried to lighten the mood. "And I'm so grateful he saved you. So—I know how, and why, you became Adam Zak. How did Nick Page become Matthew Hylton?"

Adam chuckled. "I didn't know he *was* Matt Hylton. But it's sort of my story in reverse. I was recruited into the Unit, and Fisher insisted on a name change. Tom Mercomes became Adam Zak. Nick went AWOL on the Agency and decided he'd better become someone else. I think he's used a few names, but to me he's just Wingman. Until this moment—and, I guess that memo—I was the only other person who knew they were one and the same."

Dreu looked at him incredulously. "He jumped ship on the CIA?"

Adam shifted forward as if he were about to push himself up out of the chair. "He stayed in the Air Training Command for a year after I went to the Academy to teach. Just before his discharge, he got a call from Langley. His dad was a pilot for Jordanian Air. An American. But his mother was from Jordan. As you can see, he looks Middle Eastern. Grew up speaking Arabic at home. The CIA was just waiting around for him to leave the service. He was immediately assigned to Clandestine Activities and sent to Syria. That's where he got himself into trouble."

"Was outed?"

Adam shook his head cynically. "No. You remember the uprising in Daraa? The city in southern Syria where all hell broke loose after a dozen schoolboys were arrested and tortured for spreading anti-government graffiti around the city?"

"Part of the Arab Spring uprisings," Dreu recalled.

"A very minor part. The government and army seriously over-reacted. Nick had become pretty deeply imbedded in some important circles in Damascus and thought Bashar al-Assad was one of the more tolerable despots in the Middle East—and a damn sight better than any alternative was likely to be. He strongly advised the State Department to urge the Syrian government to back off. Get the army to lighten up. Show some accommodation to the fact that these were just kids trying to act like some of the rebels in other places they were seeing on TV. And there were early signs that the Syrian government was going to do it. But there were influential people in the US, both in Washington and in the political donor community, who saw this as an opportunity to get rid of Assad. Nick was ordered to stir up trouble in two cities north of Damascus known to be anti-government strongholds: Homs and Hama. Part of his assignment was to eliminate a popular opposition leader. A man named Homsi. He refused. The Agency brought in another guy to do the job. And you basically know the rest of the Syria story. Ten years of chaos and thousands of lost lives.

"By *refused*, you mean he just disappeared?"

"Yup. After the order, they didn't hear from him again."

"So, what happened to him."

Adam shrugged dismissively. "He became someone else. Dropped off the radar. And the Agency has been trying to find him ever since. He knows too much. We contact each other periodically, just to check in." He chuckled to himself. "We use burner phones like a couple of criminals. Once to call, and again to text a number when we get a new phone. Always as Cyclops and Wingman. He never tells me where he is. I had no idea he was in Zambia."

A change on a monitor to Dreu's right drew her attention. She quickly scanned the news article that filled the screen.

"*Whew*," she whistled through pursed lips. "It looks like the Agency is only part of your friend's problems. I think it may be *his* turn to need a wingman."

3

Matt had insisted that before doing anything else, they cover the plane. "They shouldn't be looking for us yet," he ventured. "And not in this direction. But we don't want someone to overfly the area and spot it."

Taylor hadn't been quite ready to hide the fact that they were stranded in the African bush, especially when no one knew where they had been going.

"How are we going to get out of here?" she had demanded before she was willing to leave the aircraft. "Does the radio still work? Maybe we should call for help and tell someone where we are."

Matt had unstrapped his harness and pushed open the pilot-side door. "Listen," he said sharply. "Yesterday you were worried that if we got caught, we'd spend the rest of our lives in a Zambian prison. Do you think that's changed? Angola won't want anything to do with us if they pick us up. They'll send us right back to Lusaka. Who knows what the Zambians will do? I'll take my chances hiking out of here."

"To where?" she asked, throwing her arms up and looking desperately around them. "Which way do we go? And how are we going to keep from dying of thirst or starving to death—or being eaten up by whatever's out there?"

Matt held up the chart. "We're along one of the tributaries of the Lungwebungu River. It snakes around a lot, but starts somewhere in the general direction of Kuito. We follow the riverbed until it ends, then head west. Sooner or later, we have to hit a road that will take us to Kuito."

"And if we run into people first?"

"We tell them we're trekkers, lost in the bush, and ask them how to get to Kuito."

"You haven't said anything about water or food—and wild animals."

"I always keep enough food in the back of the plane for a couple of weeks, just in case something like this happens. Water? Hell, we're right next to a river. And we have two weapons and a lot of ammunition. If we set ourselves up right at night, we should be okay. We can get out of here."

She sat hunched in the seat, working through the alternatives as color slowly returned to her face. She decided there weren't any good ones, and it paled again with resignation.

"Better get busy," he said. "We'll spend tonight in here getting things together. Tomorrow we start upstream as soon as it's light enough to see. But we need to get the plane covered."

With a machete that was part of Matt's emergency stores, they cut brush from the top of the wash and piled it across the yellow wings and blue upper fuselage, breaking up sharp lines and wide splashes of color that could easily be seen from the air. Then he and Taylor set about taking stock of their supplies.

"There's a sealed tub in the tail section where I keep emergency gear," he told her. "It has water purification tablets, a UV pen, matches, one of those handheld charcoal lighters, some antibiotic creams, a couple of doses of Cipro, and enough Atovone malaria medicine for both of us for two weeks. There are also enough MREs to keep us about that long."

"MREs?"

"Meals—Ready to Eat. It's military jargon. Prepacked field rations. What they used to call K-rations. But these are a little more edible. There are also a couple of water bottles and lightweight sleeping bags that can be zipped tight enough to keep snakes and scorpions out at night. With that and the weapons, we can make it through a couple of weeks. That should get us to some place safe."

Taylor drooped into one of the passenger seats and glared at him suspiciously. "Two weeks? Are you out of your mind? And you almost sound like you expected this to happen. Everything we need for a long trek in the bush. Did you think to order an extra month of my pills?"

He ignored the bite in her tone and pushed past her toward the rear compartment. "I *always* expect something like this to happen," he said coolly. "Like I told you—piss-poor maintenance on these planes. And you always carry your pills with you."

They slept in the plane's aisle that night, Matt sliding down beside her after the bags were rolled out and throwing a playful leg across her hips.

"We may as well take advantage of the last night one of us doesn't have to stay up to keep watch—and while you still have pills," he suggested playfully, twisting over to straddle her before she could wriggle into her bag.

"Are you kidding me?" she muttered. "I've been barfing my guts up all day, and we're stranded out in the middle of nowhere, for God's sake!"

He grinned down at her in the failing light, fumbling with the buttons on her shirt. "What difference does that make? There's something kind of kinky about being out in the bush—and this will be our first time in an airplane."

She shook her head in disgust. "Here? On this hard floor? With who-knows-what lurking around out there? No way."

"Ah, come on, Taylor. How's this different than the ground in that little cave you were working in?" he cajoled. "You were the one who thought that would be fun."

"That was different," she said, twisting onto her side beneath him. "We hadn't crashed in the worst spot in Angola."

He collapsed beside her back and she turned more fully away, muttering under her breath. "You may have to get used to going without. I don't think I'm going to feel much in the mood when we're sleeping on the ground with all kinds of little creepy-crawly things around."

"Maybe you can be on top," he teased, stroking her hip and nuzzling against her hair.

She pushed his hand away. "And maybe we can forget it until we get out of here. I think I'm going to keep everything on all the time and my pants tucked into my socks."

He gave a resigned shrug and slid back up the aisle onto his own bag. "Well, we'd better sleep now. I want to be moving at first light. Looking at the chart, even if we make twenty miles a day, it might take us a couple of weeks to hike out of here."

"Oh, that's just perfect," she sniffed. "Now that you didn't get what you wanted, we'd better get right to sleep so we can hike twenty miles tomorrow. How the hell did we get ourselves into this mess?"

4

The message found him in the Sicilian town of Taormina on a day when Mt. Etna was feeling irritable and showered the seaside village with fine, gray-black ash. He was on the veranda of his villa overlooking the Ionian Sea, sheltered by a wide blue umbrella from Etna's moody rain and from a Mediterranean sun that otherwise would have been unseasonably warm. Behind him, despite the volcano's bad temper, the picturesque town swarmed with tourists. They scrambled with little respect for its antiquity over the stone seating of the ancient Greek amphitheater, took morning coffee in sidewalk cafes beneath flower-draped balconies along Corso Umberto I, the granite-paved, pedestrian thoroughfare that traversed the village from end-to-end, and gawked upward, mouths agape, at the 10th century tower of the Palazzo Corvaja. A labyrinth of narrow, winding lanes insulated him from the unruly masses, and he ventured into the town center only when cruise ships were not in port.

The brief text that accompanied a scanned newspaper clipping showed only that it came from "Magnum44," but drew him immediately from the survey of international news that had occupied his morning. The message read:

Nicholas Page located in Kabwe, Zambia. Using the alias Matthew Hylton. Disappeared there yesterday piloting a Daher Kodiak 100. Accompanied by female anthropologist Taylor Dennis, age 30. Agency looking, as are Zambian authorities. As of now, no joy.

He read the message through a second time, opened the attached article from the *Times of Zambia* recounting the disappearance, and hunched forward toward the computer screen to study the photo. There he was. The scar-faced sonofabitch responsible for his uneven gait, the hitch in a jaw that had never healed properly, and burn marks on his testicles that still woke him in a cold sweat from night terrors of searing pain ripping through his body.

He closed the open applications on his computer, stood beneath the umbrella, and glared down at the turquoise waters of the Gulf of Naxos two hundred and fifty meters below, letting his rage subside to a low boil. He had been close before. Very close. But Page seemed to have a sixth sense for when the Sicilian was closing on him and slipped his grasp. This time, it would be different.

When he could feel the injured jaw begin to relax and the flush fade from his cheeks, he entered his bedroom through the sliding doors, selected a pre-packed case from the closet floor, and told the housekeeper he would be away for a few days.

He steered his Audi through the town's twisted back alleys, avoiding the amblers and tour buses that clogged the road that wound up from the bay. Another set of switchbacks, too tight for the luxury coaches, descended the cliff to an access to the A-18. Once on the main cross-island expressway toward Catania, the Audi's Bluetooth connected him to a trusted travel agent and current lover.

"Sylvie, I need to get to Kabwe in Zambia as quickly as you can get me there. I'm on my way to Catania now. Routing and cost are not an issue. But time is critical. Use the card you have on file, and let me know what you are able to work out."

"Away again on one of your short-notice jaunts," she said with a clear note of irritation. "You make it very difficult for me as a travel agent—and frustratingly disappointing as a woman who was expecting dinner with you tonight."

"I am so sorry, Sylvie," he apologized. "In my business, these things come up. And often with little notice."

"It strikes me that your business needs better planning," she said coolly. "When should I expect you back?"

"I am afraid that is uncertain. Leave the return ticket open."

"That is the one thing I have learned to expect," she muttered.

She returned his call before he reached the airport with routing on Ethiopian Airways through Rome and Addis Ababa, destination Lusaka.

"Just under 6,000 euros," she announced in a tone that suggested she had made little effort to spare him expense.

He laughed into the Audi's Bluetooth. "Ah, Sylvie. You are such a darling. See what kind of car rentals you can find for me in Lusaka. No—better yet, find a service that will provide a car and driver by the day. I will need to go to Kabwe, so search out a good room for me there, if such a thing exists."

Her voice was now icy. "Will there be anything else, Sev? Some local companionship, perhaps?"

"We'll save that until I return," he chuckled and cut her off, but not before hearing her mutter in Italian, "You should be so lucky!"

5

Adam's flight took him from Phoenix to JFK, then through Nairobi to the Zambian capital of Lusaka. His passport showed a clean-shaven angular face, hazel eyes, and neatly trimmed auburn hair that he now wore pulled back tightly into a ponytail. The name on the passport and other documents and credit cards he carried showed him to be Robert Solomon. According to an official-looking photo ID and badge, he was a representative of the United States National Security Agency.

He booked a first-class ticket, hoping for comfortable sleep during a good part of the twenty-six hours he would be in the air. Despite the personal compartment and fully reclining seat, he slept fitfully, his mind unwilling to let go of his parting conversation with Dreu and the challenges of a search he could still not clearly define.

He had known as soon as he read the article from the Zambian paper that he had to go, and that it needed to be immediately. According to the release, the National Police Service had launched a countrywide search for the two missing Americans on suspicion of attempting to remove treasures from an anthropologic dig in violation of national and international antiquities law. American scientist Taylor Dennis, assistant team leader at an excavation in the Broken Hill Mine region south of the city of Kabwe, had failed to return from a flight to Mozambique where she and the team pilot, Matthew Hylton, had gone for supplies. The search was initiated when team leader, Dr. Alexander Phipps of the British National Museum, notified police that the plane carrying the pair had failed to return and had never reached the port of Nacala on Africa's east coast.

Several members of the team reported their suspicion that Dennis had failed to disclose discovery of skeletal remains consistent with those of the historic 1921 Broken Hill skull or Homo heidelbergensis. They believed she was attempting to smuggle them out of the country. Mr. Hylton had been serving as both security guard and pilot for the team and was said to have developed a romantic relationship with Miss Dennis. Police believed he may be complicit in helping her remove the artifacts. There had been no sighting of the missing Kodiak since it left Kabwe early Tuesday morning for the Mozambique port city, a thousand kilometers to the east.

"It looks like the CIA isn't the only agency looking for your friend," Dreu had said grimly. "The national police in Zambia are after him, and officials in Malawi and Mozambique as well."

Adam had printed a copy of the article, then headed for the spiral stairs that descended to their apartment below. "I've gotta go," he called back to her as she pushed away from the console to follow. "I owe him, and this is too big for him to handle alone."

"Adam," Dreu called after him, "this happened Tuesday. Even if you can get out this morning, he'll have been gone three days when you get there. How will you be able to find him before the police and Agency people get to him?"

Adam had disappeared down the staircase and his reply echoed up from below. "If he wants to keep from being found, he will. He's been doing it for the past ten years. But I can think like he does. They can't. And I'm not about to sit here and read memos about the hunt when I should be there trying to help him do whatever it is he's trying to do. He saved my life, Dreu, and I owe him this."

She caught up with him in the bedroom where he already had a case on the bed and was piling in clothes. "I'll need an NSA ID," he said as she entered. "Can you find that one for me? I think the Robert Solomon set will be perfect for this. It needs to be something the Agency guys won't want to challenge if I run into

21

them. And can you see what gets me into Lusaka the fastest? I'll need to stay in Kabwe tomorrow, but only book one night." He had turned to find her glaring at him from the doorway. Her voice was both accusing and pleading.

"You said Hungary was your last operational mission. This sounds suspicious from the start, Adam. If he's this antisocial type, is he the kind of guy who'd fall for some anthropologist he was supposed to be guarding? And would he help her try to take some bones out of the country? I mean, how could they possibly think they can get away with something like that?"

He straightened beside the bed and frowned into the carpet between them. "All good questions. And I don't know the answers to any of them. He's smart as hell. If anyone can figure out how to get out of there, he can. But he's also not what you'd call a guy who's comfortable around women. He had serious acne as a teenager. It scarred his face so badly he's always been pretty withdrawn, which could explain the social issues. He always seemed a little desperate for female attention, but didn't know how to handle it when he got any."

He chuckled to himself, still studying a spot on the carpet between them. "I talked him into doubling with me and a couple of girls I knew to an officers' club party when we were new flight instructors. He spent the evening staring at this girl with a stupid grin on his face. I don't think he said ten words." He looked up and shrugged. "Could that cute little woman in the picture talk him into helping her with something like this? I suspect so, if she played him right. But my guess is he may have had some other reason to think it was time to get out of there. He's been moving every three or four years since he jumped ship in Syria, just to keep the Agency off his trail."

"Which means he's been able to keep ahead of them without your help," she argued. "And you promised . . ."

He shook his head slowly. "Dreu, this isn't a mission. This is personal. It's like learning that you were in trouble somewhere.

Nothing could keep me from trying to get to you. And I need to go now."

Her jaw tightened and she also looked away. "So now that Nita's gone, I run the Unit by myself. You know this wasn't ever part of the deal." Dreu had been drawn into Unit 1 as a replacement for a woman who had served from its beginning as its tech guru, a Cuban Latina named Anita who had stayed with them and active in their work into her late eighties. Then, one morning, she had not come to breakfast. True to her request, they had taken her ashes back to be scattered behind the rural home near Ashburn, Virginia, where she had spent her life supporting and loving the original Fisher. Now Dreu Sason provided that support, including a deep and passionate love for Adam Zak.

"You were doing virtually everything before Nita passed," Adam reminded her. "And you don't have to run the Unit by yourself. I'll take one of the satellite phones and will check in every day. Lee is out of Korea, and it looks like Manny will make it into Turkmenistan today. None of the team seems to need special help right now. If they do, we can provide it from wherever I am as well as if both of us were here."

"This was never the deal," she grumbled again, but turned to climb back to the control center where the documents were kept.

"You'll need to get your hair cut," she called over her shoulder. "You are supposed to be NSA, and Robert Solomon has short hair."

Adam knew as he recalled the conversation that she was right. This *hadn't* been his agreement with the woman he now loved as much as life itself. He had promised her that he would stay out of the action, and this was likely to get messy—messy enough that Nick would need help from both of them.

He eased the reclined seat back into a sitting position and unfolded a map of the swath of Africa between the equator and the Tropic of Capricorn. Zambia was almost centered in the chart, bordered by Angola to the west, and Malawi and Mozambique to the east. Zimbabwe and a slice of Namibia formed its southern border, and the Democratic Republic of the Congo and Tanzania formed a long, twisting line to the north. During much of the colonial period, the country had been under British control as Northern Rhodesia, valued mainly for its vast deposits of industrial metals, particularly copper. The area around Kabwe had been heavily mined for lead and zinc and was still listed among the world's most polluted hazard sites. Video footage Adam had streamed while in flight showed a small city of uninspiring two-story block buildings with few trees, surrounded by corrugated workers' shanties and acres of ash and rust-colored mining waste. He wondered fleetingly where Dreu would find him a room.

As the Boeing 787 crossed the African coast and began its cross-continental leg into Nairobi, Adam googled specifications for the Daher Kodiak shown in the newspaper clipping as the plane Nick had been piloting. He was only vaguely familiar with the aircraft but knew it to be a workhorse in backcountry flying where dependability, short-field takeoff and landing were essential, and fuel efficiency a necessity. The plane had a Pratt and Whitney PT6A turboprop engine and at optimal cruise speed showed a range of 2100 miles.

Adam returned to his map, used the legend to create a paper strip to measure distance, then looped a crude circle on the chart, centered on Kabwe. Conserving fuel, the plane could reach either coast without a fuel stop, though flying west across Angola would test the aircraft's range. He did a quick search of prevailing winds in southern Africa and found that they blew east to west. Just what might make the difference if trying to stretch a flight to the Atlantic.

The stopover in Nairobi was just under an hour and Adam didn't deplane. It was 3:30 a.m. local time. His call to Scottsdale caught Dreu just finishing a pasta salad she had thrown together as an evening meal.

"In Nairobi," he reported. "Two and a half hours into Lusaka. I should get to Kabwe about ten in the morning, my time. Were you able to get a driver and place to stay?"

Dreu chuckled into the phone. "You're booked into a place called Urban Bliss. It was the best I could find in the city. If it's as good as it sounds, you can get your hair cut there. And a driver named Chuma should be waiting when you leave customs in Lusaka, holding a *Mr. Solomon* sign. What do you plan to do first?"

"Get that haircut," Adam said with a laugh. "Then I'll see if I can speak with Dr. Phipps out at the dig site. I want to know if anyone from the Agency has talked to him yet and learn what I can about the relationship between Nick and this Taylor woman. I'd also like to know what she might have taken. I think it's still possible that they headed to the coast for supplies and had trouble somewhere, though in that case, I suspect they would have been found by now. Are you picking up anything from Langley?"

"The Agency has a man in Lusaka named Pollard who has been assigned. They told him they would send someone else in to help. That second name hasn't come up yet. They may have decided to use another officer from a nearby country. Don't be surprised if they've already been to see Phipps. And be careful."

"I'm always careful," he said with a light laugh. "I'll call when I get to Kabwe. Love you, Dreu."

A middle-aged Zambian with a round face and short-cropped hair greeted him as he exited the customs and immigration area, flashing a broad toothy smile and introducing himself as Chuma.

"Ah, Mr. Solomon," he said in lilting English. "Your car is waiting. You have me for the full day. The airport is north of the city and so is Kabwe. It will not be a long drive."

Adam shook the man's hand and let him take his single bag.

Surprise arched Chuma's forehead. "This is all of your luggage? One small bag? You are not staying long?"

Adam fell in behind the driver as he led through the modern, glass-fronted terminal to a waiting area for hired transportation. As they stepped from the air conditioning of the arrival area, the sweltering heat sucked his breath away.

"Whew," he gasped, feeling perspiration instantly bead on his forehead. "I really don't know how long I'll be, but I may need to change clothes more often than I planned."

Chuma released a deep, hearty laugh and raised his free arm toward the white orb in the cloudless sky. "You will get used to it," he assured his passenger. "And it cools quickly at night."

"I'll probably be in Kabwe only a day or two," Adam called after him in answer to the man's question. "Are you free tomorrow? I may need to come back here in the morning. If your family won't miss you overnight, I'll put you up in Kabwe and pay for your services for a second day."

"I can do that," Chuma said immediately, again flashing the smile. "Your reservation said you will be at Urban Bliss. A very nice place."

"If you can call ahead, see if they have a room for you," Adam suggested. "As soon as we get there, I'd like to change, get a haircut, then drive to where the team from the British Museum has their dig. My travel agent said she thought the hotel had a hair salon."

"And a very good one," Chuma agreed. "Wash and cut your hair. Massage your head. Even give you a shave if you like."

"Sounds perfect," Adam said as they reached the car. "As long as I can get to the dig this afternoon."

"I have asked about the site," the driver said. "I know the area, and it is a cursed part of our country. Nothing will grow there now." He deposited Adam's bag in the trunk of a black Volkswagen Tiguan. Adam joined him in the front, anxious to talk to the man without having to shout across the seatback.

The drive to Kabwe followed a major highway north: four lanes of heavy traffic, still displaying the British influence of left-hand drive.

"Your name, Chuma," Adam said to break the ice. "Does it mean anything?"

Chuma grinned broadly. "It is a Chibemba name. It means 'a wealthy man.' Someone who has money. My parents must have hoped. But I have disappointed them."

"The economy is supposed to be doing better," Adam commented.

"Oh, yes," he said with a light chuckle. "But it has a long way to go. Some are getting very rich. But most of us—well, let's just say we are not Chuma."

They rode for fifteen minutes in silence, Adam noting that there were few breaks in the colorless buildings that lined the highway. As he had seen in other parts of the developing world, most had open-fronted shops on the lower level with wares spilling into the street, and living quarters above. Palms lined long stretches of the road, with gnarled, small-leafed trees spaced at regular intervals in the median between opposing lanes.

"You said this excavation site is in a cursed part of the country," he said, looking at the barren landscape behind the buildings. "What makes it so bad?"

Chumba shrugged grimly. "You will see as we get close to the city. Kabwe is surrounded by the old mines. They were closed twenty-five years ago, but the area is still nothing but bare tailings and slag dumps from the digging and smelting. The people are trying to reclaim it, but the going has been very slow. The land will grow nothing. Where they are digging—these people from Europe and America—it is out by what is called Black Mountain. It is one of the worst places."

Adam grunted an acknowledgment. "I read the city is one of the most polluted in the world."

Chumba gave a noncommittal nod. "I would not mention that when we are in Kabwe, Sir. They are working very hard. Still, I would drink only bottled water. And be certain the cap has not been broken open when you get the bottle. This was once one of the largest copper mines in the world, and a very big supplier of lead and zinc. The water supply is not safe." He paused and again grinned over at his passenger. "Still, they prefer to be remembered because of the Broken Hill Man. Is that what brings you to Kabwe?"

"Two Americans disappeared from there," Adam offered. "I'm coming to see if I can help find them."

"Ah, yes. I read about that. The government is anxious to find the woman."

"Why is that?" Adam asked, curious to know how widely the offense was known.

"They believe she has taken something they have discovered at the site," Chuma answered solemnly. "Something that might be an important treasure for Kabwe and for Zambia. It would be a very happy thing if something good was found in Kabwe."

6

They had not moved upriver at first light—at least, not far. They started: Matt carrying his rifle, sidearm, and backpack with their supplies; Taylor with the tightly-rolled sleeping bags and the pack containing the reason they could not afford to be rescued. He had opened two sealed packages of a nut and raisin mix that would serve as breakfast. With only a pale glow on the horizon, he led them toward the river, stopped after only a hundred tentative strides, then turned them back toward the plane.

"Too damn dark to be walking about in this," he muttered. "I know there are some nasty snakes in Angola, and this looks like snake country. I don't want you stepping on one we can't see—or me either. Let's get you something decent to eat and start out again when it's lighter." She stood dead-still until he passed her, peering at the shadows around her feet, then hastily fell in behind him back to the plane.

In the shelter of the fuselage, he showed her how to tuck a pouch of macaroni and tomato sauce into the heating bag supplied with the military meal, add water to the line shown on the bag, and return the packet to its box to cook. The result looked only vaguely like pasta with tomatoes.

"This tastes awful," she complained after her first mouthful. "If this is all we have for two weeks, I probably *will* starve."

He took a bite, wrinkled his chin approvingly, and took another. "Not too bad, really. And we'll get some game. But if it's all we have, it will start tasting better when you're hungry enough. Now, let me go over again what we do if we run into something that might want to do us some harm. Rule One?"

"Don't run," she grumbled, forcing down another bite of the

macaroni mix and following it with a gulp of tea.

"And if it's a cat?"

"Look big—and don't make eye contact. Don't climb a tree."

"And if we're getting water from a river?"

"Watch for bubbles and crocodile snouts. And hippos. They can run faster than we can."

"Anything else?"

"Stay away from animals in general. If baboons come when we're eating, throw our food as far from us as we can and let them have it. And stay out in the open unless we need to hide."

"Good. Now, just remember not to panic when we see something that looks threatening."

She handed him the pouch of macaroni and stuck out her tongue. "I guess I'm not starved enough yet. This is terrible. And I'll try not to panic. But if you see it first, say, 'Now, don't panic.' That will give me a minute to think before I start screaming. What if we run into elephants?"

He shook his head dismissively. "I don't think there are many left in this part of the country. They did a pretty good job of killing them off during their civil war. They're trying to re-introduce some, but not here on the east side. If any have wandered in from Zambia and we run into them, I think they'll want to stay out of our way as much as we want to stay out of theirs."

She squinted through the window of the brush-covered Kodiak. "It's getting light. Maybe we can get going. I'd like to get out of here."

He guided them back through the tangle that covered the plane and onto the broad floodplain that bordered the river. Fifty yards to their left, a steep bank rose head-high above the bare stretch of sand, topped with scattered trees and patchy thickets of brush. "If you hear a plane, head for the bush," he warned, nodding toward the bank. "Otherwise, we'll stay out here in the open." He started upstream at a brisk walk.

The only imminent danger during their first day was a sky

broken only by high, horsetail clouds and a relentless sun that baked the arid plateau. Both wore light, long-sleeved shirts, pants, and broad-brimmed hats that covered all exposed skin. But the dry, scorching air drew moisture from them as quickly as they could take it in. By mid-morning, Taylor began to falter, calling for Matt, who trudged five paces ahead, to slow or stop for longer and longer breaks.

"We can't keep moving in this heat," she complained, struggling over to one of the rare clumps of brown, wiry grass that dotted the parched sand. A wary herd of impalas emerged from the brush along the far bank, watched the pair with raised, alert heads, then disappeared back into the bush. Matt came back to squat beside her, wiping her forehead with his sleeve.

"I know this is going to be hard, Taylor" he said patiently. "But we can make it. Slow and steady. And plenty of water." He took her drink bottle and bandana and moved closer to the river where he dug a hole a yard from the slow, muddy flow of the stream with a short utility tool that hung from his pack. As the pool gradually filled, he stood and kept an alert eye on the brown, unruffled surface. With the sand filtering out sediment as water seeped into the pool, he knelt and refilled their bottles and soaked the bandanas.

"I'd rather move at night," he called back to her as he wrapped the kerchief about his neck. "But the big cats are hunting then, and the hyenas are out scavenging. I think we're safest holed up in a boma after dark, moving when the animals are hiding in the shade."

"They're smarter than we are," she called over to him. "And what's a boma?"

"Sort of like a corral. It's a ring of thorns that keeps out the critters that would like to kill us. The natives make them for their livestock."

"What if a lion jumps over it?"

"They can't—unless they want to get pretty scratched up. The thorns on the trees up there are like daggers."

"And if they don't care? If they want us more than they worry about getting cut up?"

Matt cast her an impatient scowl. "Then I guess we'd be in a bareknuckle brawl with a killer."

"Great," she muttered. "But it won't matter if we have heatstroke. It never got this hot at the dig."

"There were canopies over everything, and you were down in the caves most of the time," he shouted back at her. "We've just got to drink lots of water and walk at a steady pace."

As evening approached, he led them away from the river and onto the upper bank where he found a long-needled acacia with branches he could reach from the ground. With the machete, he cut enough to surround their bags with a shoulder-high circle of thorns, then gathered enough wood to sustain a small fire through the night. They slept in five-hour shifts, Taylor waking him every hour during her watch, certain she heard creatures slinking about just beyond their shelter.

"Unless it starts to come through, let me sleep," he grumbled after the third tug at his shoulder. She let him have two uninterrupted hours before she stirred him awake at six.

Their first encounter with cats came shortly after sunup on the second day when two young male lions appeared on the rim of the bank. Matt saw them first and slowed to let Taylor catch him. "Now, don't panic, but there are lions to the left. About nine o'clock. Keep moving at this pace and stay close." Taylor was immediately pressed to his side, clutching his elbow like a vice.

The cats ambled down the steep embankment, stood to watch the pair until they were a hundred yards beyond them, then crossed to the river. They lapped cautiously at the murky water, then trailed at a casual plod, looking more curious than hungry. Matt slowly eased his rifle, a CZ 550, from his shoulder and chambered a round.

"If they decide to get aggressive," he said quietly, "I'll drop to one knee to shoot. Get down behind me." He gave the animals a quick backward-glance. "I think they're just trying to figure out what we are. Keep moving at this pace."

"I thought they were supposed to hunt at night," Taylor hissed.

Matt used the elbow grip to steadily urge her forward. "My guess is they came to drink. They're just curious."

After nearly an hour, the lions turned away, deciding the slow, upright creatures weren't worth their time. And the morning was getting too hot.

"They're gone," Matt muttered after another backward glance. She groaned and dropped limply onto her knees.

"What am I doing here?" she whimpered. "This isn't the way it was supposed to be. We were going to fly to the coast and be on a ship by now."

Matt turned slowly, scanning the edge of the distant scrub for signs of the cats. "Well, things didn't exactly go like they were supposed to, did they?" he said coolly. "And we're a hell of a long way from the coast. So we can sit here and complain, or keep moving. At this rate, we're not going to come close to twenty miles today."

"Don't snap at me," she hissed. "I wanted to go to Mozambique, like we said we were going to. We could have made it onto a ship in Nacala before they even knew we were gone. But no! You said we'd be better off flying across this godforsaken country where no one would ever think to look for us. Now we'll die out here, and you'll be right. No one will ever find us."

"I'm not snapping at you," he said defensively. "And if you'll just keep moving, we'll get out of here without getting caught. My guess is they've already checked every ship that left Mozambique. We'd have been picked up by now."

She sniffed loudly. "Maybe I'd rather be found than get baked to a crisp—or mauled by lions."

"*Quiet*," he hissed. "And move slowly over toward the trees. There's a girl getting water up along the turn in the river."

She didn't budge. "That means there's a village. They can get us help."

"Out here, it will be a tiny village. If they have a radio at all, they'll report two white people wandering around in the bush," he countered. "If they come for us out here, we'll be in one hell of a lot of trouble. I'm not ready for that."

"But you got us these Canadian passports . . ."

". . . for when we get to where people expect to see a couple of Canadian trekkers," he retorted. "No one would be wandering around way out here. Come on. She hasn't seen us. Let's get out of sight."

They left the river for a mile, staying far enough back among the scattered brush that they could see across the floodplain, but couldn't be seen from the far bank. The thickets had thinned, and they moved easily between clumps without returning to the open sand. In late afternoon, Matt found three acacia trees close enough together to harvest branches for a new boma. Much to his relief, Taylor found the evening meal more palatable: meatballs with marinara sauce. She slept again in short fits, wrapped tightly in her bag and pressed close against Matt's hip as he took the first watch. He woke her at 2:00 a.m. She refused to get out of her bag, but scanned the area around the fire through the Kevlar window the drawstring left about her face, seeing a scorpion in every blade of bent grass and fearing a night invasion with every hoot or whistle that penetrated their ring of thorns.

7

Urban Bliss was a pleasant surprise. As they rolled into Kabwe, Adam had found the area around the city just as Chuma had described it: stripped bare of anything living, pocked by craters and rust-colored tailing heaps, broken up only by the skeletal concrete remains of abandoned smelters and crushing mills. But the hotel was tucked away on a quiet street in the heart of the city with shaded courtyards that sheltered its guests from the toxic world beyond.

"It is good that we are staying here," Chuma whispered as they entered an understated Scandinavian modern reception area. "This was built by an NGO to provide employment for the people here. These are the best jobs in Kabwe—and this is the best place."

Adam checked them in and found his room a reflection of the same standard: clean, modern, with a massage chair and complimentary fruit basket. He changed quickly into boots and khakis, spent forty-five minutes in the hotel's hair salon recapturing the look on his passport and being lulled close to sleep by the skilled fingers of a pretty young hairdresser, then met Chuma in front of the hotel's marble entry arch.

"You were right about the massage," he said with a grin. "I may have to have another trim in the morning."

Chuma laughed and nodded gratefully. "Thank you for letting me stay here." He cast a furtive glance about the parking area. "I am almost embarrassed for these people to see me here. Some of them know me, and know I am not truly *chuma*. I could never stay in a place like this."

"It is well worth having you available for tomorrow," Adam assured him, feeling a twinge of embarrassment at the man's gratitude and at his own feigned generosity. The room had cost an extra $40.

"I will willingly suffer through it for one night," Chuma added cheerfully. "Now—I will take you to a place that is not so grand and comfortable."

Black Mountain was a lifeless heap of slag that scarred the landscape northeast of the city. As the car skirted the mound to the north, a makeshift village of tents and lean-tos appeared against the bleak backdrop. Beyond the canvas encampment, a long trench had been scooped from the base of the hill. As Chuma pulled up beside the largest of the tents, a lean, ruddy-faced man with a shock of unruly carrot-colored hair pushed through the flap and stood studying the arrivals with fists planted on the hips of his wrinkled shorts. Adam stepped from the car and offered a friendly hand.

"Dr. Phipps?"

The man nodded suspiciously.

"I'm Robert Solomon from the US National Security Agency. I'm here to try to help you find your fugitive Americans."

Phipps did not take the extended hand. "You Yanks seem to have taken a real interest in these two," he said with a cultured Oxford accent. "You had two men here yesterday. Are you not keeping each other informed?"

"Ah! I gather Pollard beat me here by a day."

Phipps answered with a curt nod. "With a man named Turnley."

Adam smiled agreeably. "Two of our regional people. "They're scouring places between here and Nacala to see what they can find. I'm just in from Washington and wanted to visit the site personally. For one thing, I'm very intrigued by your work and its contribution to the chain of human evolution. I'd be interested in learning more about that, if you have a few moments. Then perhaps you can tell me what you know about our errant citizens."

The lanky Englishman's face relaxed as he accepted Adam's interest as genuine. He wrapped a calloused hand around the one his guest still held towards him.

"I'll be delighted to show you around. Some of this is still a bit hush-hush, if you get my meaning. Not ready for public announcement. But a man in your business should understand that."

"Completely," Adam nodded. "I suspect that might relate to your concern about Miss Dennis's disappearance. We are most anxious to return to you anything she might have taken. It is in all of our interests to avoid any international ill will. Perhaps a better understanding of what you are finding here will help me locate her."

Phipps waved his visitors into the tent. "I gathered from Pollard that your primary interest is in Mr. Hylton. Not in Miss Dennis."

"Very true. But we see Miss Dennis's intentions as most likely the driving force behind the couple leaving, and where they might go. Would you agree?"

Phipps nodded thoughtfully. "Most likely. Now, let me give you a brief overview of what we have here." He guided Adam through the tent to one of the canvas tarps that had been stretched between poles over a pit that cut into the base of the mound of slag. Chuma remained with a team of African workers who painstakingly picked and scraped small particles of rock from a collection of slate-gray bones.

"You are familiar with the Broken Hill skull or Rhodesian Man, I assume?" Phipps asked Adam as they looked down into the mouth of a chest-high cavity that disappeared beneath Black Mountain. Lights from headlamps chased each other across the walls of the low cavern and three female voices echoed from somewhere back in the chamber.

"Yes. Quite familiar. That's one reason I was delighted to be assigned to follow up here. The find was thought to be a critical piece of our understanding of human development."

"Quite so. The skull was found somewhere near here in a natural cave by a Swiss miner. Perhaps this very spot. Unfortunately, the site was not preserved, and further mining covered and obscured the exact location. Our excavation is an attempt to find it or other remains from the same period."

"Have you been successful?"

The anthropologist wagged his unkempt mane. "We can't be certain. We have uncovered two caves, one rather large and one quite small. Both contain animal and a few humanoid remains. The young women here are working in the larger cave. Most of what we have found here are animal bones. But we have uncovered two partial skeletons of children, probably younger than ten years old. They are yet to be tested."

"That's wonderful," Adam declared with genuine interest. "I understand one of the challenges with the skull found earlier is that it hasn't yielded any usable DNA, and destruction of the earlier site compromised your ability to date the remains. I've read dates ranging from 30,000 years to as early as 300,000 years ago. Will these discoveries help narrow that gap?"

Phipps gave him an approving glance. Here was someone who truly *did* appreciate what they were doing! "Finding these caves will help with dating," he acknowledged. "But the children's bones are unlikely to contain usable DNA after all this time and in these conditions. That is why we are so unhappy—and disappointed— with Miss Dennis." He nodded toward a smaller tarp and pit. "When we began our excavation, we worked along the base of Black Mountain, essentially digging a trench down to native rock, cutting along the face of what was once an escarpment. We have been extending that trench for four years now. This year we uncovered the entrances to the two caves. That one . . . ," he tilted his head in the direction of the smaller pit, ". . . allows only one person to work it at a time. Taylor has been with me from the beginning, so I assigned her that site."

"And she found something important," Adam ventured.

Phipps nodded grimly. "We believe so." He called down into the pit. "Evelyn, could you come up for a few moments please? There is a gentleman here asking after Taylor."

A young woman wearing khaki shorts and knee pads backed out of the cavity and stretched upright, She had an oval face with a wide mouth and large, heavily-lidded eyes. Her skin struck Adam as unusually pale for someone spending her days in the African sun. A green bandana covered most of her short, wheat-colored hair. She gave Adam a long, appraising look, then stiffly climbed the short ladder that descended into the trench. Wiping her hands on the hips of her shorts, she extended one to their visitor.

"I'm Evelyn. How can I help you?" Adam guessed the accent to be North British.

"I'm actually here with the American group looking for Matt Hylton," he confessed. "But I am aware that the two disappeared together, and it sounds as if she may have been the reason for the disappearance."

Evelyn cast her leader a quick, questioning look and received an approving nod.

"I'd say you have that right," the girl said. "She's been working on him the full time he's been here. Gave him the right treatment, she did."

"Could you explain what you mean by that?" Adam asked.

"Well, I don't know if you've been around Matthew, but he's a bit of an awkward type. Not very comfortable around the ladies, if you get my meaning. He's very self-conscious about his face. Had a bad complexion when he was young, and it scarred him up pretty badly. Oh, he's a right nice lad and all, and we all got on just fine. Very quiet. Hard to get a word out of him. But Taylor gave him lots of attention. At first, he didn't know how to handle it, mind you, but he finally decided she was really interested in him. She had a way of doling out her favors, if you know what I mean, just often enough to keep him on her leash. I had the feeling he hadn't really ever had a woman give him what he thought was that kind of affection, like, and he was testing her to see if she was truly into him."

Adam nodded. "And *was* she genuinely interested in him?"

39

Evelyn looked quickly again at her supervisor. "That's a hard thing to say, isn't it? We were all suspicious, I can tell you that. When Taylor got here this year after our break, she talked a lot about someone back home at university. We all thought she was pretty serious about this bloke. Then she started giving Matt all her attention."

"This friend from the university. Do you remember a name?"

"Wesley, I believe. I don't know that she ever told us his last name."

"And when did the interest in Matt begin?"

"When she started getting back into that cave."

"And you think it was related to what she found? And to this disappearance?"

"After they didn't come back, we all thought so. She was really protective of the work she was doing. Wouldn't let any of the rest of us in there. She said it would 'mess things up.' She photographed a lot of animal bones and they were, like, arranged like they'd been put there. Set out in some ritual way. She didn't want any of that disturbed."

"But no humanoid bones?"

"Well, that's just the thing, isn't it? She brought out two fragments. A piece of sacra. A short segment of what we think is tibia. That cave has stayed drier, for some reason, and these fragments are better preserved. So why not more? We thought, just among us, that she might be setting some aside somewhere. Dr, Phipps was about to talk to her about it, but then they didn't come back from that supply run. They disappeared."

Adam turned to the anthropologist. "Is that true? You were planning to confront her?"

"I couldn't imagine her hiding specimens she was finding," he said glumly. "But the girls seemed certain. She made a habit of coming out for lunch and breaks after the rest of us were in the tent. She could easily have hidden some things away without being seen. I was going to talk to her after she came back. We think she must have taken what she was hiding with her."

Adam glanced over at the smaller excavation. "What would she gain by taking them out? You operate in a small professional circle. She can't do anything with them without being discovered."

Phipps followed his gaze toward the cave. "We've been in there since. Up along one wall is what looks like an area that may have been chipped out to create a shelf for a body. There are still stone fragments scattered about the floor. The shelf would have kept remains drier and out of contact with bacteria-bearing soil. The jewel in the crown in this profession right now would be viable DNA from a specimen of Homo heidelbergensis. If she found a skull in there or some of the larger bones of an adult, this might be the best opportunity we have had to recover DNA."

"But again," Adam objected, "how could she do this without being discovered?"

The British scientist's face furrowed. "Miss Dennis is a most ambitious young woman. Perhaps being discovered is what she wishes. I can imagine her running the tests, revealing the results, and immediately returning the artifacts to Zambia. I would be most surprised if your government chose to punish her."

"Wouldn't it ruin her professionally?"

Dr. Phipps frowned thoughtfully. "I doubt there is a comparison in your profession, Mr. Solomon. But does the name Leakey mean anything to you?"

"Of course. The Leakeys did some of the most important pioneering work here in Africa in human evolution."

"Well, then suppose a successful DNA test does what many of us suspect it might do. Fill the genetic gap between Homosapien and Neanderthal. If your name could be forever linked to that discovery, what price would that be worth to you? I suspect some wealthy person might be willing to fund further research for you, even if a university or museum wouldn't. Especially if you had returned the specimens."

Adam gave the man an understanding nod, thinking as he did

that in his profession, the objective was to remain *unknown*. "But as far as we can tell," he mused, "it doesn't appear the couple made it out. Any thoughts as to what happened to them?"

"If I had to venture a guess," the doctor said, "I would say they arranged to land somewhere before they reached Nacala and bribed someone to hide them."

"And the plane?"

"Yes. And the plane."

"Did you suggest that possibility to Pollard and Turnley?"

"I did. Mr. Pollard said they have offered a ten thousand dollar reward for information leading to discovery of the plane or of Mr. Hylton. They thought that might tempt anyone hiding the plane to come forward."

"Unless that person was given the plane as an incentive to hide them," Adam suggested. "Then, $10,000 isn't much of a prize. But as I said, our people are now systematically working their way toward the coast, checking every little airfield."

"That is what I would be doing," Phipps agreed.

"Thank you. And thanks to you, Evelyn. You have both been most helpful. We'll see what we can do to recover your bones."

He found Chuma back in the team tent carrying on an animated conversation with one of the workers.

"Back to the city," he called to the driver. "We need to leave early tomorrow to drive to Lusaka. And I may need your help chartering an early flight to Zambezi."

"There is an early regional flight to Zambezi," Chuma said. "But one of the men was just telling me the people who are lost were flying to Mozambique. Zambezi is in the other direction."

Adam grinned over at his driver. "Yes," he said. "I know it is."

8

The man from Taormina did not ask his driver's name. It was not his nature to become too familiar with those he hired to work for him. But he did offer the man an extra fifty euros a day if he would hang around with the chauffeurs in the lot outside Urban Bliss and learn what he could about other guests and why they were in the city. Then the Sicilian stayed out of sight. If all went as expected, in a few days he may be in another place where he did not wish to be recognized as 'that man who was at the hotel in Kabwe.'

His driver was a genial man who knew all of the other chauffeurs, knew how to get them talking with his own easy banter, and desperately wanted an extra fifty euros that he wasn't required to split with the rental company. Late in the evening after other guests had deserted the lounge and bar, he and the cheerless man with dark eyes and thick, wavy hair the color of coconut shell drove north for half an hour along the T2 toward Ndola while he reported his discoveries of the day. His passenger listened without expression, asked a few questions, and let him know when he should return to the hotel. The return drive was in complete silence, ending with the European handing him a 50€ note as he exited the car.

The second evening, the driver knew his fare would be especially pleased. He waited until they passed the outskirts of Kabwe, then carefully watched his passenger in the mirror while he recounted the day's happenings.

"Three of today's new arrivals are with NGOs," he began. "All are here to work on reclamation projects. They spent part of the morning touring the waste sites, but most of the day in meetings."

The man behind him gazed absently into the dark night as if not even listening to the report.

"The fourth driver took his passenger out to the same place on Black Mountain where the two Americans went yesterday," he continued, seeing the man's attention quickly shift inward. "The place where the people are digging for old bones. That driver, a man named Chuma who I know well, said his passenger is also American. He told Chuma he is looking for the man and woman who disappeared in their airplane. They spent an hour at the dig site asking questions about them." He waited for a response, but none came.

"As they were driving back to the hotel, the American told Chuma that tomorrow morning they would go back to Lusaka. The man is flying from there to Zambezi."

"Where is Zambezi?" his passenger asked.

"Over on the west side of the country. Near the border with Angola."

The dark-eyed man straightened in the seat, then leaned forward. "Not toward Mozambique?"

"No. You know the Zambezi River? Victoria Falls? The river is on the very far side of Zambia. The city with the same name is along the upper river. Near Angola."

"You can turn around now," his passenger said, sliding back against the seat. They returned to the hotel in silence, the man fingering his cell phone during the entire drive. As he climbed from the car, he handed the driver a 100€ note. "Be ready to leave at five o'clock in the morning," he ordered. "We will be driving to the airport in Lusaka."

9

Late in the morning of the third day, they reached a bridge. Formed concrete piers supported eight sections of metal grating that spanned the river high enough above the floodplain to survive the erosive power of sudden spring flash floods. The track on both sides was no more than parallel ruts in red, hardpacked clay.

"I think we should follow it," Taylor suggested, standing between the tread marks and gazing longingly in both directions. Her soaked shirt clung like shrink wrap, showing ribs that were becoming more prominent with each MRE she tossed aside after a few, begrudging bites.

"Which way do you suggest we go?" Matt asked, following her eyes as she turned.

"You've got the map," she answered irritably. "And you're the big bushmaster and security guard. You tell me."

"If this appears on the chart at all, it leads to some little place called Lucusse. That way." He pointed across the bridge. "Maybe a day away. But if we go there, we're asking for trouble. We need to stay away from people as long as we can—at least until we get nearer to Kuito. It's the kind of city where trekkers won't attract a lot of attention. But we will out here. Unless you want to end up in a cell with nothing but a bowl of *shishima* to eat every day, we need to stay out of sight."

"What the hell is *shishima*?"

"That white mush stuff the poor people around Kabwe ate all the time." He tossed her a glare that was his first visible sign that patience was running thin. "Oh, excuse me!," he muttered. "You probably didn't ever meet any poor people in Kabwe."

"Okay, smartass," she sneered, swinging her pack from her

shoulders and dropping it at her feet. "And how far are we from Kuito?"

"Maybe another week, depending on what kind of time we make. We haven't had a twenty-mile day yet, so it may be more like ten days."

"Ten more days in this hellhole?" she scowled. "I'm starving to death, my feet are killing me, I'm getting blisters from these pack straps, and you don't give a damn."

Matt swung his own pack to the ground. "Hell. I've felt like a damn cheerleader trying to keep you from getting so down and discouraged. If I remember right, what you wanted me to do was get you out of Africa and back to your precious lab where you could test those bones you've stolen. If you want to turn yourself in, be my guest. Just head that way." He pointed across the metal span. "Take whatever you want, Taylor. Take all the MREs if you think you can force them down. And I'll let you have the Ruger. Maybe someone will come along and pick you up before you reach a town. I've done everything I can think of to get you out of here safely and keep you out of jail. But that's made me part of this. And I'm going that way." He nodded off into the bush to the west.

Taylor's face flushed crimson. "You'd leave me here by myself? Whatever happened to 'Oh, I love you, Taylor? I'll help you get your precious bones back to the States.' Every night you were happy to have a good lay but now, when I want to get us to someplace we can get help, it's 'Sorry. You're on your own. I'm going that way.'"

"I *am* trying to get you back to the States with your damn bones," he said with a dark look. "You always seemed to like the sex as much as I did until something didn't go your way. Since then, you haven't had any trouble saying no. And since we left the plane, I've gotten used to leaving your precious bones pretty much untouched. Aside from that pair of lions, we haven't seen anything that would hurt you if you head off on your own. Stay on this track and you'll probably be okay. But I need to tell you, I'm not sure this road goes to Lucusse."

"Damn you," she snarled. "You crashed the plane, and now you want me to hike in this heat for another week? I can't do that. Not without better food."

He stood on the faint track and frowned at her for a long moment. "How about this?" he suggested finally, glancing up at the sun. "Let's get down under the bridge in the shade. We just passed a herd of duiker that were moving in this direction. I'll see if I can get one. We'll stop for a few hours. We can cook up a good antelope shank. Once your belly's full, you might be able to think straight."

"You said we shouldn't be shooting things and butchering meat."

"I think using the rifle isn't smart. Sound carries out here. And so will the smell of blood and fresh meat. But I'll risk a shot if it will keep you happy. I'll cut off a shank and leave the rest far enough away that if it attracts scavengers, they won't bother us. Then we can move another couple of miles before we stop for the night."

She glared at him sullenly for a long moment, looked again across the river, then off into the bush beyond the road. With an exaggerated groan, she stooped to pick up her pack. "Okay. If we can find a place under the bridge with no lizards or snakes, you can go see if you can shoot something. But don't bring it all back. Just what you want to cook. And you'll have to take care of cutting it up and fixing it."

"I'll get some wood and start a fire before I go," he agreed. "You can feed it so we have good coals when I get back. But I'd like to get away from this road and a few miles farther along before night."

"Then you'd better get all this done in a hurry," she grumbled.

The duikers, small, humpbacked antelope with spindly legs, had been moving slowly after them along the upper bank. He found them after ten minutes, grazing unconcerned fifty yards into the bush. A .357 round wasn't ideal for the small animals, but he was confident he could hit one in the chest and wasn't concerned about preserving more than a hindquarter. He stretched prone at the edge of the embankment, sighted on a young buck, and dropped it with a clean shot just behind the front shoulder. The herd scattered in three directions, leaving the dead animal in an open patch of cropped grass.

Matt dragged the carcass another hundred yards farther into the bush and severed a hindquarter with his knife. He hacked off the lower leg and, keeping a watchful eye for predators he knew could smell fresh blood half a mile away, sliced away a square of hide, wrapped the section of rump in the skin, and detoured on his way back to the bridge until he found a thicket of straight-stemmed bushes with pale, butterfly leaves. With the machete, he hacked off three branches, two forked at one end.

Taylor sat with her knees tucked tightly against her chest, moodily feeding the growing pile of coals.

"I think you're being selfish and way too cautious," she muttered as he dropped the bundle beside her and began to prop the Y-shaped branches opposite each other across the fire. "If we hike into that town and find a public bus or something, nobody's going to think anything about it. There were people coming in and out of Kabwe all the time."

He sharpened the straight stick, unwrapped and skinned the rump section, and began to work the spit through the muscle along the bone. "This isn't Kabwe," he argued. "Any town out here is going to be small and isolated. Their first question will be 'Where did you two come from?' Unless, of course, they've already been alerted to watch for two Americans wandering around lost in the bush. And this isn't Zambia. Angola isn't exactly a major destination for trekkers—especially this part of the country. If we can get to Kuito, it's big enough that we can disappear into the city."

"Yeah. *If* we can get to Kuito." She wrinkled her nose at the raw chunk of meat. "Is that likely to have parasites in it?"

"Nothing that cooking won't kill," he answered coldly. "And I told you, you're welcome to head on up the road any time you want. I'll give you the MREs to take along. I'm going west."

10

Adam waited until just before turning in to call Dreu. It was 10:30 in Kabwe. Early afternoon in Scottsdale. As promised, he had called her just after arriving in Lusaka, but she still sounded relieved to hear his voice.

"There's a lot of interest inside the Agency in what's going on over there," she told him after a quick exchange of *I've missed you's*. "They have two people working their way toward the coast, checking every airfield to see if Nick and his friend landed somewhere before reaching Nacala."

"Pollard and Turnley," Adam said.

"You've run into them?"

"Almost. The people at the dig told me they'd been there the day before. It was pretty easy to guess that's what they'd do next."

"So they've got a bit of a jump on you."

Adam chuckled. "I don't think so. I believe they're looking in the wrong place."

"Tell me," Dreu said simply.

Adam leaned back against the pile of pillows. "It does appear they're right about Nick letting this Taylor Dennis talk him into flying her out with something from the excavation. I think I know him well enough to be pretty certain he'd head for one of the coasts. But he'd try to go some direction they wouldn't expect— like west."

There was silence, and Adam knew Dreu was bringing up a map. "You mean, across Angola?" she asked after a moment. "Could he make it that far in whatever he was flying?"

He relaxed farther back against the headboard. "That's just it. Most people wouldn't think so, and most pilots wouldn't try. It's about eleven hundred miles from Lusaka to the closest places on the Atlantic. The Kodiak he was flying has a max range, fully loaded, of just over a thousand."

"It doesn't sound to me like any sane pilot would try it," Dreu muttered.

"Well, I checked the specs on the aircraft and if *not* fully loaded and flying low at what they call economy cruise speed, he could stretch that range to thirteen hundred miles. With no wind, that would get him there on fumes. I checked the wind charts, and the prevailing currents here blow east to west. On the day he left, he would have had a tailwind of about fifteen knots if he stayed low."

Dreu was again silent, and he gave her a moment to study her map. "That's a long coastline," she said finally. "Where would he head?"

"Again—trying to think as he would, I'd take the shortest route to a small, general aviation airfield. I'd want to be fairly close to a major port. I think they probably booked passage on a freighter or tanker of some kind—with a captain who, for the right money, would take a couple of extra passengers on board and not ask questions."

"You're making a lot of assumptions, Adam."

"Not as many as you might think. They're doing a pretty thorough job of looking east. I'm quite certain he wouldn't go north into the Congo, or south to Botswana or South Africa. The Agency will have calls out to every place he could land there. I'm pretty sure he went west."

"And why wouldn't they have calls to places west?"

"They might. But not on the coast. They wouldn't believe he could make it that far."

"Then Nick and that woman might be on one of those container ships right now," she ventured.

His voice became more solemn. "That's just it. I don't think they made it, and I don't think they landed at an airstrip. I spent the last hour calling every field of any size between here and any place

51

he could reach on the Atlantic. None had a Kodiak land with that tail number."

"So what do you plan to do?"

He paused, then said, "Dreu, I know I'm betting everything on this hunch, but I'm flying in the morning to Zambezi over on the west side of Zambia. What I'd like you to do before I get there is chart a line between Lusaka and Benguela on the Angolan coast. It's the port city he had the best chance of reaching, and they have a small, general aviation-type airport. Then get high resolution satellite images of the area in between for the day before Nick left and for two days after. Have your computers create a strip twenty miles wide along that line, and ask them to compare the two days. If you haven't been exaggerating about what your little wonder machines can do, they should be able to pinpoint anomalies between the sets of images."

"I can do that. What kind of resolution do you want? If we get too fine, even large animal movement will show as anomalies."

"Eliminate anything the size of an elephant or smaller. We're looking for a plane that's thirty-five feet long and has a forty-five foot wingspan."

"I believe I can get that done by the time you get to Zambezi."

"And do something else for me, if you would please. See what you can find out about Taylor Dennis and a guy named Wesley."

His morning flight to Zambezi was on a Kodiak, a plane that aside from color and number was identical to the one he was trying to locate. It was outfitted for nine plus the pilot, with limited luggage space behind the rear seats. Adam was one of six passengers: two Australian couples bound for a safari lodge north of the city along the river, and a single Italian of about his age who could have stepped out of a 1960s safari movie.

"I've bagged about everything but a giant sable antelope," he boasted to the Australians as they waited to board. "Not a lot of them left, and they are protected in Angola. But some are rumored to have moved across the river into Zambia where they are not protected. We're going to see if we can find one for my trophy wall."

The Aussies whispered among themselves about why someone would want to hunt down one of the last remaining animals of its kind, a sentiment Adam shared. He asked the young African pilot, who introduced himself as Joseph, if he could take the copilot's seat. The trophy collector struck him as a man who would use the captive audience of the closed cabin during the hour-long flight to detail earlier hunting exploits. It would be best if mounted heads of sables, elephants, and black rhinos didn't come up again with Adam close enough to comment.

"Are you a pilot?" Joseph asked as he leveled the plane at seven thousand feet and saw the man beside him studying the instrument panel.

Adam grinned across the center throttle console. "Many years ago. Military pilot. Lost an eye in a flying accident and haven't flown much since." He tapped with a finger below his left eye. "You lose your depth perception with only one of these. It makes it much harder to land."

The pilot nodded, casting a curious glance at Adam's eyes.

"Do you enjoy flying this plane?" Adam asked. "Like the way it handles?"

"Ah, yes. Very much."

"A good reliable aircraft?"

"Yes. I have never had a problem."

"If you did, could you put it down pretty easily out in the bush?"

The pilot laughed. "I don't believe we will need to try. But if I can find five hundred meters of open space, I can do it."

The airfield in Zambezi gave truth to Joseph's claim. Two short dirt strips formed a brown X in the middle of a town that nestled on the high, arid plateau beside the Zambezi River. Joseph eased the Kodiak down onto the longer of the two and taxied to a plain, single-room adobe building. The only other aircraft in sight was a Bell Ranger helicopter with *Upper Zambezi Tours* emblazoned across its side over the silhouette of a bull elephant. Adam guessed it to be the chopper he had chartered.

As the Kodiak braked to a stop, an older man with a mop of gray hair and weathered black skin stepped from the airfield building. He watched the six Caucasians deplane, recognized four to be couples and a fifth to have a car waiting, then strode cheerfully toward Adam.

"Mr. Solomon? I am Nelson. You have chartered a tour for today?" The man's shake was strong and confident.

"Call me Robert, please. And yes. Your people said you would be able to cross over into Angola. Did I understand that right?"

"Oh, yes. We fly both directions along the river looking for wildlife. If we go very far north, we are in Angola."

"I need to make a call," Adam said. "Then I'll be ready when you are. I have a somewhat different interest than spotting game. Are you open to leaving the river on this trip?"

Nelson shrugged. "You have booked the chopper for the afternoon. I will take you wherever you would like to go with the time and fuel we have."

"Very good. Do you know the Angolan side well?"

Nelson grinned broadly. "I *am* Angolan. I came here during the war. I know eastern Angola as well as any man you can find."

"Then I've found the right one," Adam chuckled. "Let me make my call. I'll join you at the plane."

Dreu answered on the first ring. "I almost tried to call," she said before he could ask what she had learned. "But I decided you'd get in touch as soon as you could talk safely. Are you in Zambezi?"

"Just landed. You sound like you found something."

"Several things. All important." Her voice was excited, but tense.

"Start with the plane."

"I think I found it. There is one major anomaly on the second

54

set of satellite images. It's about sixty miles west of you on the south bank of the Lungwebungu River. Something is filling the end of a wash that opens onto the river. It's well covered with brush, but it could be your airplane."

"Can you give me coordinates?"

Dreu read a series of numbers."

"How close is that to the flight path we guessed?"

"Almost at its center. And it's the only spot along the route that showed significant change over that three-day period."

"Good work, Dreu. I love a woman who knows how to manipulate computer images the way you do!"

"I hope that's not all you love about me," she grumbled. "I still haven't forgiven you for leaving me here alone. I didn't realize how much we're missing Nita. She would have enjoyed this little project. It makes me nervous."

"She trained you well," Adam assured her, ignoring the "left alone" complaint. "What else have you got for me?"

Her voice took on a more secretive tone. "You asked me to check on Taylor Dennis. A couple of especially interesting bits of information there. First, everyone describes her as extremely ambitious. 'Driven' was the word a couple of people used. I got the feeling she isn't universally liked. But more importantly, you asked about a Wesley. She has had a serious male friend at the university for the past two years. Serious enough that some called him her fiancé. And he took a leave of absence a week ago. Unspecified length. No one knows where he went. But a female colleague guessed he might be planning to meet her somewhere."

"Hmm," Adam murmured. "Also good information. What's his last name?"

"Epling. Wesley Epling."

"You might want to plug Mr. Epling into international departures and see if he shows up anywhere. If he does, I'd like to know where he's going."

"Already done," she said. "Waiting for results."

"Thanks, Dreu. Is that it?"

"No—and this last item worries me, Adam. I'm intercepting reports that Pollard and Turnley went back to the excavation site when their search didn't turn up anything. Dr. Phipps mentioned your visit. They contacted the Agency to see what they could learn about Robert Solomon with NSA. We had created that file in their database, but Pollard was suspicious. He had the Agency call NSA and confirm. And of course, they said they didn't have a Robert Solomon and hadn't sent anyone. But Phipps remembered your driver's name was Chuma. They're trying to find him. Did he know you were going to Zambezi?"

Adam swore under his breath. Stupid mistake. He'd been out of the field too long. "I'm afraid so," he confessed. "They'll learn pretty quickly that we were at the Urban Bliss and that I put Chuma up for the night. I suspect he put address information in Lusaka on his registration. They will track him down."

"Then you probably only have a day's lead on them, Adam. Who's taking you to look for the plane?"

Adam had walked to the corner of the airfield building and glanced over at Nelson who was doing a final walk-around of the helicopter. "A guy with a chopper tour service here," he told her. "Upper Zambezi Tours."

"You might start thinking about how you can keep the Agency guys from finding him very quickly," she suggested.

"Any ideas?"

"I'll bet he'd be interested in the reward for finding the plane I see mentioned in the Agency memos."

Adam chuckled. "And I also love a woman who's a step ahead of me all the time. Better go. Love you!"

He tucked the satellite phone back into a leg pocket of his pants, pulled his standard cell from a shirt pocket, and studied a map of eastern Angola.

"Do you own this chopper," he asked Nelson as he tossed his pack into the open side door of the Ranger.

"No. It is owned by a company in Livingston. They mainly offer tours along the lower Zambezi and at Victoria Falls. I am the only one who does tours here."

"Are there other tour companies who fly out of here?"

"No. We are the only one. This is not a big safari area."

"Would they object to you extending our tour to three days and to you going to Luena in Angola?"

Nelson shrugged. "I do not see why they would object—if you pay up front. I can call them."

"Why don't you do that. Have them add the charge for the extra days to the card I gave when I booked the flight. Do you know Luena?"

Nelson again grinned slyly. "I told you, no one knows eastern Angola like I do. I am from Chicala, very near there. But do you plan to land in Luena? If we leave the plane, you must have a visa. And if we do not return today, you must have a pre-booked reservation in Angola."

Adam paused beside the door of the chopper, sizing the man up. Helicopter pilot. Probably late 40s. From rural eastern Angola and claiming to know that part of the country well. Left to come to Zambia. There was a good probability that Nelson had been a UNITA rebel fighter during Angola's long civil war—a man who knew how things could get done along this remote stretch of frontier without too much fuss.

"And how might I get a visa on very short notice—and without a reservation in Luena?"

Nelson wagged his head noncommittally. "The airfield manager can issue a visa under special circumstances. A tourist visa is generally eighty British pounds. That would be about one hundred US dollars. A special circumstance visa might cost a hundred fifty—and perhaps something for me for explaining your special circumstance to the manager."

Adam gave him a knowing grin and nodded toward the airfield building. "Okay, then. If extending the tour is alright with your company, tell the man in flight operations that we would like to go to Luena under special circumstances, and will be gone for three days. I'll give you two hundred dollars. Then, I have a proposal for you that can make you considerably more than an extra fifty bucks."

Nelson cocked his head suspiciously.

Adam raised a reassuring hand.. "All legal, I promise you."

"Will you be coming back to Zambezi with me?"

"Possibly. Probably not."

"Your Angola itinerary must show where you plan to leave the country."

Adam considered the complication for a moment, then said, "If we don't return here, I will probably leave from Benguela."

"Benguela! I cannot take you that far," Nelson objected.

"You will not need to take me farther than Luena," Adam assured him. "And there is no risk to you in the proposal I have for you. If we can get the visa, I will explain it in the air."

11

"Everything I want to do, you think is a bad idea," Taylor shouted at Matt, who was a dozen paces ahead and now carried the bedrolls strapped to the top of his pack. He stopped and waited for her to catch up, eyeing a family of four jackals that had been staying parallel to them where the bank steepened above the floodplain. The day was again cloudless, the sun relentlessly charging the bare sand of the riverbed with heat that rose around them like a dry sauna.

"Two reasons for that," he said as she stopped a few yards from him and wilted onto her knees. His tone was mockingly patient. "The first is that what you want keeps changing. You wanted me to get you safely to the coast with those damn bones. Half of Africa has to be looking for us, but at the first little road we came to, you wanted to head for a village. Sorry, but that's not going to get us out of here safely."

She glared off at the jackals who seemed to worry her less than the shirt that clung to her like a T-shirt in a Florida beach contest. Pulling up the top of her water bottle with her teeth, she took a long slurping drink, then forced the container roughly back into the pocket on her pack.

"The second reason is that you keep wanting to do things that will get us both killed. Yes—we're both hot as hell and we both stink. But we can't climb into that river. We've seen crocs along the bank, and they'd be on us in a minute if we start splashing around in there. And I didn't want us carrying the rest of that meat because I don't want us smelling like dinner to animals like those jackals over there." He paused for a moment, then said less patiently, "Anything else?"

She looked up sullenly. "You took my phone. There's probably no signal out here, but at least I could try to call someone and let them know we're alive."

Matt sniffed. "I told you, they'll be watching that number like flies on shit to see if you call anyone. They can track where a call comes from to at least the nearest tower. And anyway, where the hell do you think you're going to get a signal out here?"

"Then why not give me my phone?"

"Because who knows? They may have towers scattered around so there's contact with villages."

"And you don't trust me not to call."

"If you're not going to call, you don't need the phone. And we need to save what juice is left in them for when we *do* want to call."

"I need to get washed," she pouted, looking down at the soggy shirt.

"If we find a smaller stream that empties into the river, we can wash. Something too small for the crocs to be hiding in."

"And if we don't?"

"If we don't, we stink. But I'll make you a deal. I think we're about forty or fifty miles from a town called Cuemba. When we get there, we'll see if we can find a place to get cleaned up and catch a bus to Kuito."

She sneered up at him. "So, all of a sudden it's okay to go into a town?"

He turned to face the jackals that sat on their haunches watching the pair. "No," he muttered. "I'm just getting really sick of all this bitching."

Midway through the afternoon they came across the remains of an abandoned surface mine. River water had seeped into a shallow pit the size of a backyard swimming pool that Matt could see was clear of predators. They stripped off their sweat-drenched clothing, threw them into the pool, then eased into water that was bathtub-hot from the relentless sun.

Taylor stretched along the sandy slope of the pit's edge, water up to her chin. "I'm staying here for the rest of the day," she announced. "You can rinse the clothes off and hang them somewhere. I'm not moving."

He splashed over toward her in the chest-deep pool, grinning down at her naked body and making no effort to hide his arousal. "Maybe I can help you wash, and we can check those bones out again," he said, arching his brows suggestively.

She rolled onto her side against the slope of the pool. "Not a chance," she muttered. "I'm worn out. And I hate that shaggy beard close to me, dirty or wet." Since he had suddenly decided he needed to grow a beard, she had complained about it daily and it seemed a perfect excuse at the moment. As bad as it felt to have that cratered cheek against hers, she had learned to tolerate it. The beard? She absolutely loathed it.

He didn't argue but stood a few yards away, studied her with what she would have recognized as sadness had she been looking at him, then turned and fished their clothing from the water. He sloshed them enough to rinse out the sweat, then tromped naked across the sand to two twisted I-beams that jutted from the hard ground, wringing them out as he went.

"Those steel things are going to stain," she shouted from the pool. "Stretch mine out on those rocks over there."

He looked toward the only mound of rocks within sight and the striped wild dogs that hovered above them, then threw the clothing over the rusted metal. "You're going to have to live with a few stains," he announced, and plodded back to his side of the bath.

As evening approached, they dried in the late afternoon sun and climbed back into their sunbaked gear. The mining operation covered the outer bank of a wide sweep in the river where the floodplain stretched for what Matt guessed to be a half-mile from the main channel.

"I don't see any trees," he muttered. "We'd better head

upstream and see if we can find something thorny to build our boma before it gets dark."

"Nothing's been bothering us here, and we're a long way from the bush," she argued. "Maybe we could just stretch out by those metal things tonight and wash again before we leave in the morning."

He scanned the area about them and shook his head. "Not a chance I want to take. Especially with these jackals watching us."

"What if we walk till dark and still don't find a tree to cut up? Then we'll be in closer to the bush and still won't have one of your boma things."

He turned slowly, scanning a horizon that didn't give him reason to think she was wrong. Beyond the pool they had bathed in, a horseshoe shaped trench had also flooded; deeper and wider than the smaller pit, with a narrow neck at the open end of the loop.

"We'll camp in there," he said, pointing at the sandy peninsula. "Let's get our packs over there and see what wood we can find. If it's driftwood, make sure it's good and dry. The fire's going to be the only thing that keeps animals out."

The creatures of the night sensed an opening. Though Matt built their fire across the narrow neck that was the only way onto their protective island and kept it sparking and crackling through the night, the jackals closed in after sundown, pacing restlessly just beyond the flames. The day's trek and warm bath had sapped the last of Taylor's strength, and she slept with long, noisy breathes behind the flaming barrier. Matt sat at its edge, a round chambered in his rifle and the Ruger beside him on his bag.

Just before midnight, the night erupted with a chorus of grunts, groans, yelps, and whines that sent the jackals running toward the distant bush and Taylor bolting upright. She tore at the bag she had tightened around her face, finally freeing her hands to strip it to her ankles. Matt scrambled to his feet and began to pace behind the fire, letting the animals see him through the flames.

"What is it?" Taylor whispered hoarsely, stepping free of the bag and pressing close against his back. The grunts broke into a string of giggles and growling laughs.

"Hyenas," Matt hissed. "As long as they see us moving, we should be alright. They usually don't like to attack anything that will fight back. But if they think we're wounded or dead, they'll be in here in a second, ripping a chunk out of us."

"Even with the fire? Can they swim?"

"I don't know. But I'm not going to find out."

"Shoot one!" she yelped, seeing the first of the hunched, grinning beasts slink into the edge of flickering firelight.

"If I kill one, they'll tear it apart right there. I don't want the smell of blood to bring anything else down here that doesn't care if we're moving around and doesn't mind getting wet."

She stepped back and pulled the empty bag back up over her shoulders. "So, what do we do?"

He grabbed a stick the size of an axe handle from the flames and hurled it toward a second spotted animal that had crouched into the circle of light. It jumped back, but was immediately replaced by two others, heads low and eyes gleaming yellow. "We keep moving around until it gets light," he muttered, knowing it wasn't going to be "we."

The hyenas slunk away when the first trace of dawn paled the eastern horizon. Matt watched, bleary-eyed, until it was bright enough to scan the sandy stretch of river bottom and see that they were gone. Taylor had remained seated upright in her bag during the first hour of yipping and growling laughter, then slumped back to the ground with the bag tightly about her ears and slept fitfully. He stooped and shook her shoulder.

"They're gone. I need you to get up and watch while I catch an hour of sleep. I'm pretty well wasted and won't be worth anything today if I don't get some rest."

She struggled out of her bag. "What do I do if they come back?"

Matt pulled off his boots and stretched out on top of his bag. "They're pretty much nocturnal," he mumbled. "Keep the fire going and just watch for them. If they come back, wake me up. And wake me in an hour anyway. We haven't been making very good time and need to be moving." Before she could ask more, he was asleep.

12

When the airstrip disappeared behind them, Adam handed Nelson a slip of paper and pointed west. With Nelson's permission, he had taken the seat beside him and pulled on the copilot's headset.

"We're not going directly to Luena," he said through the intercom. "Put these coordinates in your GPS and head there. It's somewhere along the Lungwebungu River. It will take us a little south, but not too far out of the way."

"There is nothing out there," Nelson objected. "Not even villages. They mined there before the war, but did not find the diamonds they thought would be there. Now there is nothing."

"There is something, and it can be worth half a year's wages for you. Have you heard about the American couple who disappeared a few days ago on a flight from Kabwe?"

Nelson gave him a suspicious glance. "I heard of this. From my company people. They sent helicopters from Livingston to help with the search. But the people were going to Mozambique."

"That's what they told everyone," Adam confided. "But they came west. Listen—what I am going to tell you will sound unlikely, but it's God's truth. And there can be a lot of money in it for you, if you help me."

Nelson screwed his mouth into a skeptical frown, but continued toward the coordinates. Adam decided he would have to trust that his pilot had once been a UNITA rebel.

"The man who is missing with the aircraft is an old friend," he told Nelson. "A man who saved my life when I had an in-flight emergency years ago. He spent time later with the American CIA in Syria, but disappeared after he refused to assassinate a rebel leader in an American attempt to stir up opposition against the government."

Nelson stared intently at his instruments, the frown deepening.

"I learned he had disappeared about the same time the CIA did. They did not know he was in Africa until they saw news of the plane being lost. Two of their men have been sent to find him, but he doesn't know he has been discovered. I am trying to get to him before they do." Adam paused, letting the African digest what he was hearing. Nelson eased the chopper down to skim the tops of the acacias and a few, scattered baobab trees as they approached the watershed of the Lungwebungu.

"Has this man contacted you?" he asked.

"No. As far as I know, he and the woman haven't been in touch with anyone. They may be dead."

"But somehow you know they came this way instead of going to Mozambique."

"Were you a military pilot?" Adam asked.

Nelson looked over at him cautiously, then nodded.

"Did you fly with anyone you trusted like a brother? Someone you felt you knew as well as you know yourself?"

Nelson didn't have to consider the question. "Yes, I did."

"Well, I knew this man that well. He would create an escape plan no one trying to find him would think possible. And let's just say I have access to the same kind of intelligence information the CIA does. An associate was able to get satellite images of the route this man would have taken if he'd headed west—toward places on the Angolan coast he could reach if he really maxed out the aircraft. She found what she thinks is the plane. At those coordinates."

Nelson stared thoughtfully at the numbers he'd set into his guidance system. "And you think he will be alive if the plane is there?"

"My colleague said it looked like the plane had been covered with brush. I believe they are trying to hike out."

Nelson slowly shook his head. "There is nothing out there. They could not have chosen a worse place to go down."

"Or a better place," Adam suggested. "They weren't looking to be found."

"What are you planning to do if they are trying to trek out?"

Adam grinned over at him. "That's where my proposition comes in. There is a ten thousand dollar reward for information leading to discovery of the plane or the people. If we find the plane and they aren't there, my guess is that Nick—that's my friend—will try to stay out of sight for as long as possible. He'll keep moving west, probably following the river, but will avoid roads and villages."

Nelson sniffed skeptically. "That will not be difficult. There are no roads and very few villages. It is surviving that will be difficult."

"If you had to track them, how would you go about it?" Adam asked.

Nelson's brow knitted thoughtfully as he eased the chopper to a safe altitude and studied a chart strapped with a Velcro belt around his left thigh. "Lucusse," he said finally. "I know a man in Lucusse who is a hunting guide and the best tracker in Moxico Province." He grinned over at Adam. "He knows Eastern Angola almost as well as I do, but from the ground. These coordinates are not far from Lucusse. If your friend is not with the plane, we can go there and see if he will help."

"Sounds like just the man I need," Adam agreed. "So, here's my proposition. If we find them with the plane, you take us all to Luena, wait there for two days while we find a way to get to the coast, then fly back to Zambezi and report having located the plane. No mention of finding the people. You say you left me in Luena, then went down to search along the Lungwebungu because I thought it might have been their route. You collect the reward."

"And what do I say happened to you?"

"Tell them I went on toward the coast, which will be true."

67

"And if we don't find them?"

"If it's clear they left the plane, take me up to Lucusse. I will try to hire your tracker friend. You can then drop us back along the river, then go back to Luena. Wait there another day, return to Zambezi, and report finding the plane. Same plan."

Nelson nodded. "But why must I wait in Luena for two days?"

"The CIA men will know about me by now. It will take them about a day to learn I came to Zambezi and that I hired you. I need to stay at least two days ahead of them. Once they learn where the plane is, they'll have a pretty good idea where we're going. Just not what route we took."

"They may want help from me," Nelson worried.

"Don't offer any information, but fly them wherever they want to go," Adam suggested with a sly grin. "No one knows Eastern Angola better than you do."

Nelson dropped the Bell Ranger to fifty feet above the brown surface of the river and slowed enough to barely keep them aloft while Adam scanned the left bank.

"There!" he said sharply, pointing across to the pilot's left. Had Dreu's coordinates not placed them within yards of the image on the satellite photos, he would have missed the concealed Kodiak, mistaking it for a tangle of brush swept to the mouth of the wash by a sudden storm.

Nelson powered up and rose above the water, circled back over the gray tangle of limbs, then back around to settle the chopper onto the sand. Adam waited until the rotors were still, climbed with the African from the Ranger, and cautiously approached the hidden aircraft.

"Nick!" he shouted. "It's Cyclops." Nelson looked over suspiciously. Adam gave him a dismissive shrug. "Lots of names in this business," he muttered. There was no answer from the plane.

The interior showed the remains of a meal eaten in the passenger area. An emergency storage case was empty, aside from a few items cast aside because of weight or questionable utility: a small fire extinguisher, life jackets, a folding metal mess kit, and a ten-liter plastic bucket. Nelson picked up the mess kit and released the snap, examining the utensils and folding cup inside.

"I would think they would take something like this," he mused.

Adam held up an empty MRE packet. "Looks like they have a supply of prepackaged military meals," he said. "Everything will be included in the packets. The kit was extra weight."

"Can I have it?" Nelson asked.

Adam turned back toward the door. "Help yourself to anything you see—or wait until you come back and find the plane. I have no idea how they'll get this thing out of here." Nelson followed with the extinguisher and two of the life jackets.

Adam ducked from beneath the brush and walked back toward the Ranger, inspecting the ground. "Clear sets of prints left in the direction of the river, turning upstream. Looks like they went west," he said to Nelson. "And they've got a four-day lead on me. Let's get over to Lucusse and find your guide. Then maybe you can take us up-river as far as your fuel allows, see if we can pick up their tracks, and gain some ground on them."

Nelson turned back toward the Kodiak. "First, I need your help," he said. "If I am going to discover this plane from the air, more of it must be visible. We should at least uncover the tail."

As they pulled long, thorny branches away from the rear of the aircraft, three dark-striped antelope with long twisting horns stepped from a thicket of trees on the bank above. The men paused, watching the wary animals until one bolted out of sight and the others followed.

"Were those Angolan sables?" Adam asked. "I understand some have survived over on this side of the country and a few have wandered into Zambia."

"Those were kudu," Nelson said dismissively. "There are no sables here and none close. The few that remain are in Cangandala National Park. It is hundreds of kilometers from here."

69

Adam tossed aside the branch he was holding and looked warily at the chopper pilot, a deep furrow creasing his brow. "Are you certain about that, Nelson?"

"Very certain," the African said, grasping another thorny limb and throwing it away from the plane. "They are the national animal of Angola. Very important to us. And if any had been found in Zambia, we would have heard about it. They would guard them like they do the black rhino. But you can ask my friend in Lucusse. He is the best hunting guide in eastern Angola."

Adam didn't answer. He was filing a mental note that when he next spoke to Dreu, he needed to ask her to find out who else might be hunting the endangered Nicholas Page.

13

It was unusual, Marshall Pollard acknowledged, for station chiefs to be doing as much legwork as he and Justin Turnley were doing in this search for Nick Page aka Matt Hylton. Both were chiefs with few Indians: Marshall working out of the embassy in Lusaka and Turnley in Botswana. Neither had more than two direct reports within the embassy, with other in-country CIA operatives posing as representatives of various American enterprises in the countries. And both were intelligence officers in nations with little intelligence to be gathered. It was clear that finding the former Page was an obsessive interest of key officials within the Agency, and the search provided more excitement than either of the men had experienced since receiving their appointments. Both were delighted to leave the confines of the embassies and do some boots-on-the-ground fieldwork.

Pollard was the picture of a diplomat, though all within the embassy, and most in Zambian governmental circles, knew that his official State Department title was a very thin veneer covering a spy chief. He was a trim man in his late fifties with distinguished salt and pepper hair, a neatly trimmed mustache under an aquiline nose and gray, penetrating eyes. Those close to him knew that his soft-spoken manner disguised a perceptive mind that missed little. He had known Turnley since the two served as station officers in Kenya and welcomed the suggestion from Langley that they pair up in the search for Page.

Justin Turnley's roots, five or six generations in the past, were Tswana, linking him ethnically to three-quarters of the people in the country he now served. In a well-tailored suit, he could stroll through the streets of Gaborone and be indistinguishable from

Botswana's burgeoning class of successful businessmen. He spoke two dialects of Bantu and, at forty-five, was a rising star in the Agency's southern African constellation.

Following their initial meeting with Alexander Phipps, the men had conscripted the help of Pollard's junior officer. Within a day, the three managed to contact every airfield between Lusaka and the Mozambique coast. With each in a separate chartered plane, they visited fields that had the luxury of hangar space, reassuring themselves that Page and Taylor Dennis hadn't arranged to hide the Kodiak where it couldn't be seen from the air. By evening, each was convinced the fugitive Americans had not flown east. Their second trip to the excavation site turned the search, at least in Pollard's mind, into much more than a manhunt.

"So, the NSA says they've sent no one down here—and that they don't have a Robert Solomon," he repeated back to the head of Clandestine Activities during his call to Langley. "This man was described as six-one or six-two, slender, athletic build. Brown hair. The professor in charge of the project here said he noticed something different about his eyes. Thought one might be artificial, though a very good one. The man seemed unusually well-informed about both the excavation here in Zambia and about Matt Hylton." Pollard listened intently to his CIA boss, then concluded with, "He stayed at the same place we did, a hotel called Urban Bliss. We have learned who his driver was and are certain we can track him down. We'll keep you posted."

The hotel had an address in Lusaka for Chuma. As the late afternoon sun began to fade over the city, they found the simple, metal-roofed home on a dusty back street in the northwest suburb of George. It stood a dozen steps across a yard of grassless dirt, surrounded by a broken wooded fence. Pollard stayed in the car, watched suspiciously by a dozen barefoot boys in shorts and T-shirts who kicked a soccer ball back and forth across the dusty road in the dwindling light. Turnley had changed into a pair of dark trousers and a plain, short-sleeved white shirt. He spoke pleasantly to the boys in Bantu as he pushed through the sagging gate and rapped on the door. The man who answered acknowledged that he was Chuma.

"My name is Justin Turnley," the CIA man said. "I am from the American embassy. May I have a few minutes of your time to ask about Mr. Robert Solomon?" Chuma studied him for a long moment, then stepped aside and ushered him into a spare sitting room furnished only with a tattered sofa, two wooden chairs, and a low coffee table holding a small flatscreen TV.

"May I serve you coffee?" Chuma asked as Turnley took one of the armless chairs. In an adjoining room, the CIA officer heard others whispering softly, but no one joined them.

"No. I don't wish to disturb your evening, but believe you can help us. You drove Mr. Solomon to Kabwe and back earlier in the week. We are trying to locate him. Can you tell me why he went there?"

"You say you are Mr. Turnley?" Chuma repeated. "You have been to the place in Kabwe where I took Mr. Solomon. I heard the Englishman there mention your name."

"Yes. That's right," Turnley improvised. "Did he tell you why we had been there?"

"You were looking for the two Americans who disappeared—like Mr. Solomon. He said you were working together to find them."

"Solomon said that?"

"Yes, Sir. He knew a Mr. Pollard had been there. The Englishman told us you were with Mr. Pollard."

"Mr. Solomon mentioned Pollard by name?"

"Yes, Sir. He said you were part of their regional people."

"Hmm. And you brought Mr. Solomon back here? To Lusaka?"

"I did, Sir. I brought him back to the airport."

"Do you know where he was going?"

Chuma frowned suspiciously. "You do not know where your own man went?"

Turnley leaned forward, elbow on knees. "That's just it, Chuma. Mr. Solomon is not with the US government. We don't know who he is or why he is interested in finding the missing couple. Did he happen to tell you?"

Chuma slowly shook his head. "No, Sir. We did not talk about it."

"Do you know where he went?"

"No, Sir. I just dropped him at the airport Tuesday. He had only one bag. I thought maybe he was going back to America."

By the time Turnley returned to the car, the street was dark and the boys had abandoned their game. He slid into the passenger seat beside Pollard.

"We've got a problem," he said grimly. "This Solomon knows who you are and that you're looking for Page."

"He told this to Chuma?"

"No. Solomon mentioned you by name to the Brit at the dig."

Pollard stared intently at the lighted windows of the simple home. "Does he know where Solomon went?"

Turnley shook his head. "He claims he doesn't know."

"Do you believe him?"

"I really don't know," Turnley murmured. "But I do believe him when he says he brought him back to the airport. He said he thought Solomon was headed back to the US."

Pollard nodded in the dark. "We may need the help of the local police in the morning. We need to check the manifests of every flight going out of Lusaka that morning. Solomon will be on one of them, and I'll bet my pension he wasn't going back home."

14

The tracker's name was Yander. He was a small man, but tough and sinewy as the gnarled trees of the dry plateau on which he hunted. Adam guessed that he and Nelson had once fought together, though neither mentioned the civil war that had left the country in ruin.

"Yes, I will help you find the man," he said in English after a short conversation with Nelson in a language the helicopter pilot said was Chokwe. "But you must be outfitted. Come with me. There is a shop in the town where I take my hunters." An hour later, they were airborne with Nelson, following a road that led south from Lucusse. Adam carried a light pack and bedroll and a Ruger Hawkeye 30-06 that he guessed had once seen action in the country's war.

"Take us to the bridge," Yander shouted to the pilot over the loud *thump-thump* of the rotors. "If they followed the river, we will find signs of them at the bridge. We will see if they continued west, or took the road."

Twenty miles south, Nelson settled the Ranger onto a long span of metal grating that crossed the Lungwebungu. Yander was out and moving toward the far side of the bridge before the rotors stopped, trotting in the low crouch of a man who had experience exiting a chopper on the move. Adam followed him down off the road onto the sand where the hunter pointed at sets of tracks that cross-hatched the riverbank.

"They were here—and they made a fire under the bridge." He led Adam beneath the span to where two stout sticks still stood beside the remains of a campfire. The wiry African shook his head critically. "They are not trying to hide their tracks. They will be easy to follow."

The men returned again to the road, walked a hundred paces away from the bridge with Yander studying the packed surface, then dropped down again to the sand on the west side.

"See here," he called to Adam. "They did not take the road. I think they do not wish to meet anyone." He shouted up to Nelson who watched them from the metal span. "Take us up to the old mine. We will see if they made it that far. If we find signs of them there, you can leave us. You will need your fuel to get back to Luena."

Thirty minutes later, Nelson lowered the Ranger over a wide bend in the river that had been turned into what looked like a battle zone of craters and tailing mounds. Adam spotted the black scorch on the neck of sand surrounded by the flooded horseshoe trench. "There," he shouted over the rotor noise, pointing down at the dark circle. "Another campfire." Nelson circled and brought them down beside a smaller water-filled pit. This time Yander surveyed the ground through the open door of the chopper before jumping to the ground.

"They spent time in this water," he said, nodding toward the pool. "Then camped over by the fire."

While his guide slowly circled the smaller pit, Adam started toward the remains of the campsite.

"Wait," Yander called after him, freezing him in his steps. The hunter moved slowly toward him, studying the ground between them. "They had company," he announced. Adam followed the point of the man's rifle barrel but saw nothing.

Yander tilted his face into the white glare of a sun that now bore straight down on them. "The sand is firm here and the sun is high. The worst time to see tracks. No shadows. But look here. A pack of jackals. And over here, hyenas. That is why their fire is surrounded by water."

"They must have escaped," Adam observed. "I don't see any sign they were attacked. And Nick would be armed."

"Yes. They left here," Yander agreed. "But these are spotted hyenas. They are more aggressive than their brown or striped brothers. If they have not found something else to kill, they will follow and attack."

They returned to the Ranger, retrieved their gear, and watched as Nelson lifted off and turned north. Yander carried a rifle and small canvas pack that contained a thin tarp, water bottle, fifty rounds of ammunition, and fire-starting materials. A crude scabbard stitched to its back held an 18-inch machete, with a shorter knife strapped about his waist. He had insisted Adam carry no more, assuring him that they could find what they needed in the bush.

"We will want to move fast," he had advised. "All we need is water, fire, and some way to kill food and defend ourselves. Everything else is extra weight."

As the chopper disappeared, he bent again over the smaller set of human prints. "These people are not moving fast," he announced. "The woman walks with heavy feet. We should be able to find them by tomorrow—if you can stay with me." He looked up at Adam, flashed a challenging grin, and started upriver at a steady trot.

15

Pollard and Turnley touched down in Zambezi shortly before three in the afternoon. Getting police help to comb through flight manifests of passengers departing Lusaka had been more complicated than either had expected. Pollard eventually called the US ambassador, who had in turn called the Zambian head of the national police. The American diplomat had explained that the information was critical to the search for the missing Americans from the Kabwe dig, and to returning any stolen artifacts to national authorities. It had taken another two hours to dig through the stacks of manifests, find Robert Solomon on the Zambezi passenger list, and charter a plane to follow.

Once in Zambezi, they had found flight operations to be managed by an ancient man with ash-colored hair and jaundiced eyes who said his name was Fanwell. When first questioned, the name Robert Solomon didn't seem to ring a bell with the man. While Pollard circled the building looking for some means to get beyond the river town if their search required it, Turnley politely pressured the old field manager who sat back loosely in a swivel chair behind a cluttered metal desk.

"You have heard of the disappearance of the two Americans on a flight from Kabwe?" he began. "We are involved in that search and are working with the cooperation of the national police. Do we need to bring them out here to see if it improves your memory?"

The manager shuffled through his scattered papers, running his rheumy eyes over them nervously. "I am willing to help you, but I do not know the names of all the people who come through here."

"And how many might that be in a day?" Turnley pressed.

"Some days eight or nine. Some days, only three or four. But these foreign names are hard to remember."

"And yesterday?"

The man gazed absently out the single window that opened onto the airstrip. "Yesterday? Six people."

"Yes. Two couples, and two single men. One was Robert Solomon."

"Oh, yes. I remember him. He had arranged for a charter tour."

"To where?"

"The pilot said they were going into Angola. To Luena."

"And has the pilot returned?"

The manager shook his head slowly and gave a long, drawn out "Nooo. He said they may be gone for three days."

"Is there another charter I could get to Luena?"

"Nooo," the man said again. "Not until Nelson comes back. That would be tomorrow. And others may already have the helicopter booked."

Turnley walked to the window, watched Pollard cross irritably in front of the building, then turned again to the field manager. "How far is Luena? Can you rent a car around here?"

"Yes, there is one place. But he will not allow his cars to go into Angola without a driver. And Luena is about four hundred and seventy kilometers. Seven, maybe eight, hours to drive. And you will need a visa. For a short term visit? Two hundred American dollars."

Turnley swore under his breath. "How do I get a damn visa?" he wondered aloud.

"I can help you with that," the man offered. "But I would check first on a car rental. You do not want to pay two hundred dollars and find that you cannot go. And if you can go, I would do it tomorrow. If you are going to stay overnight in Angola, you must have an advanced booking. If you wait until tomorrow, perhaps Nelson will be back and can fly you there if no one else has booked a flight."

"Do you have a number for the car rental place? And a

suggestion for a place to stay?"

"It is the same place. A lodge along the river." He dug a card out of his desk drawer. "If he has someone who can drive you tonight, for a fee we can arrange a reservation in Luena. But I would wait until tomorrow."

The owners of the River Horse Lodge, a young transplanted South African couple named Kellerman, offered a two-bedroom cottage for the night and agreed to free up a driver after the morning safari tours.

"Our trucks go out at six and are back about nine, depending on what there is to see," Ethan Kellerman explained. "You might call the airfield when we have a driver available and see if Nelson is on his way back. It will be no more expensive to fly, and you can get there in a fraction of the time. If you get a short-stay visa, there's no need to advance-book a room. Over and back in one day. And it will help us to have our driver here for the evening excursions."

The Australian couples who had flown into Zambezi with Solomon had both checked into the lodge. After the late-afternoon safari run, the CIA men primed them with drinks and mined them for information about their flight companion. A man who introduced himself as Marc remembered Solomon's interest in the plane.

"He asked to sit up with the pilot, seemed familiar with all of the instruments, and asked a lot of questions about what would happen if something went wrong," Marc remembered.

"It made me right nervous," his wife, Claire, said in her broad Australian accent. "But our pilot was happy to talk to him about it. They were two men who both knew a great deal about flying." The couples excused themselves, explaining that a 6 a.m. game tour meant a 5:20 wakeup. The CIA men moved out onto a veranda overlooking a broad sweep of the river.

Pollard sipped thoughtfully at a gin and tonic and watched a family of warthogs trot warily to the edge of the water and kneel on their front legs to drink.

"Do you see any reason NSA might have someone here and not tell us about it?" he asked Turnley, who had propped his long legs across the cushions of a free chair.

"Not tell Langley? I doubt it," Turnley said.

"Then, if this Solomon isn't with us and isn't NSA, who is he?" Pollard pondered.

"I've been wondering the same thing. He seems to have better sources of information than we do. Some other country's intelligence group? Syrian or Israeli?"

"Possible," Pollard said skeptically. "But I think both would be perfectly happy letting us take care of our prodigal son."

"So you think he's American?"

Pollard nodded and sipped at his drink. "Have you ever heard of Unit One?" he asked his partner.

Turnley shook his head. "No. Not that I recall."

Pollard was silent for a moment, then said, "When I was stationed at Langley, there was backroom talk about a small, deep-cover operation that had been around almost as long as the Agency. According to the gossip, only the director and the president know about it, and they aren't even sure who's in it."

Turnley chuckled skeptically. "That's hard for me to imagine. They wouldn't let some maverick outfit operate with no oversight. I mean, we have covert teams that take care of the really sensitive stuff. Why would we need something like you're talking about?"

"Well, let's suppose," Pollard mused, propping his own heels up on the railing, "that we got involved in something that was dangerously illegal or contrary to our national interest. Who reins us in?"

"What we do is always supposed to be in the nation's interest," Turnley challenged. "Give me an example."

"You recall the rumor a couple of years back that there was a lethal virus on the global market, and we had a team trying to acquire it?"

"Yes. I heard something about it. Despite the veil of secrecy, word gets around."

"Well, we didn't get it and whoever did was intercepted and the virus destroyed. The internal whisperings were that it was this Unit One group who believed no one should have it. They saw our interest in acquiring it as a violation of the biological weapons treaties."

"We were probably trying to get it to destroy it anyway," Turnley argued.

Pollard regarded him with a wry smile. "You honestly believe that?"

Turnley shook his head dismissively. "Even so, I can't see why the director or president or anyone would put up with this mystery team meddling in something like that."

"Perhaps because they also do things that have to be done that we can't—like removing candidates like Graves and Mehrens from contention in the last election before either ruined the country."

"You're not suggesting . . ."

"That was the office talk. "

Turnley arched a dubious brow. "How does this Unit One get all its information?"

Pollard shrugged. "They are linked into the Langley computers. Have access to everything we do. And the theory is that they've kept their equipment more state-of-the-art and have a couple of tech geniuses who can squeeze blood from a stone."

Turnley stretched back, letting the possibility simmer while he watched the warthogs disappear, replaced by a solo giraffe. Finally he asked, "And you're suggesting this Solomon might be a member of this unit?"

Pollard set his glass on the slatted bamboo tabletop beside his chair. "I'm just trying to come up with an explanation. It's a bit disconcerting to have someone we can't identify staying two steps ahead of us. And he has to know we're following him."

"But why would these Unit One people care about Page?"

Pollard ran a finger around the rim of the glass. "Do you know Page's history? That he disappeared from the Agency because he thought we were making a big mistake in Syria? There are a lot of people now who would agree with him. He refused to make a hit that he knew would lead to civil war and apparently tipped off the rebels that one of their leaders, a man named Homsi, had been targeted. The covert who took Page's assignment and managed to get to Homsi was captured and tortured pretty brutally before the US got him back through a prisoner swap. The Agency's been trying to find and silence Page ever since to keep him from embarrassing us with what he knows."

"You mean, that the whole Syria thing might have been avoided if we'd paid attention to our own intelligence?"

"That's basically it," Pollard agreed.

"I remember the swap," Turnley muttered. "The guy's name was Messina, if I remember right. Whatever happened to him?"

Pollard shrugged. "Again, rumor has it that he was pensioned with a pretty sweet deal to keep him from going public with the same information."

"And you think this Unit One team is trying to save Page?"

"Maybe after he left us, he became one of them."

Turnley rocked forward in his chair. "And maybe this Solomon really *is* NSA," he suggested. "They may not believe we can get to Page and aren't willing to tell us they sent someone down who they think can do the job. We can ask when we catch up with him."

After an impatient breakfast, waiting for drivers to return who had chosen to extend their morning game tours because elephants had been sighted along the river, Pollard called the airfield to see if there was any word from the helicopter pilot.

"As a matter of fact, he just called in," Fanwell reported. "He said he's on his way, but is swinging south to have a look at something one of the fixed-wing pilots called about, but couldn't stop and check out."

"Did he give you an ETA?"

"He expects to be here before noon."

"Excellent," Pollard said. "I'll call his company and arrange a flight to Luena as soon as he can get turned around. When one of these drivers can bring us to the airstrip, we'll be there to arrange visas."

"I'm sorry, Sir," the field manager said, "but there is another gentleman here who has already contacted the company and booked the helicopter."

"What do you mean, booked the helicopter? We said we might be needing it."

"You told me you may be driving. He had also asked about it earlier and is already here and has paid. And I must remind you, I am not the tour company."

"Is he there with you?" Pollard demanded. "Let me talk to him."

Another voice came through the phone. "This is Eraldo Manco," the man said. "How may I help you?" His accent sounded Mediterranean.

"I have something of an emergency that requires my partner and me to get to Luena in Angola as quickly as we can today," Pollard explained, then briefly described the hunt for the missing aircraft with his two countrymen. "Could you possibly delay your tour another day? We will happily pay for it and any other expenses the inconvenience creates," he pleaded.

Mr. Manco chuckled softly. "As it turns out, I am not touring. In fact, I am going to Luena where I can catch a flight farther west. I would be happy to have you join me if you wish."

"Wonderful," Pollard exclaimed. "This is so generous of you. We will cover the flight costs for you."

"Anything I can do to help you find your countrymen," the man said. "I am hoping to leave as soon as the pilot can refuel."

Ethan Kellerman had been at the registration counter while Pollard made the call. "I take it you are going to the airport and won't need a driver," he said. "I'll run you into the city myself."

Pollard nodded his thanks and walked through the sliding doors onto the veranda where Turnley waited with their bags.

"The chopper's on its way back," he told his partner. "That damn Fanwell let another guy book it, but it turns out he's also headed to Luena. We reached an agreement to share the ride. Ethan will run us out to . . ." He was interrupted by the young South African who hurried after him onto the covered porch.

"Fanwell called again from the airfield," he said with enough urgency to stop the agent in mid-sentence. "Nelson called from about a hundred kilometers out. He says he has discovered a plane in the bush. He thinks it might be the one you are searching for."

16

The Sicilian had asked his driver to stop within sight of the airstrip until he saw Robert Solomon lift off in the Bell Ranger, then returned to the flight operations building.

"I see that one of the people I arrived with was able to book a helicopter," he said to the old man whose primary function seemed to be to sit idly on a rough-hewn bench in front of the adobe building and stare absently down the airfield, waiting for something to jar him out of his hazy stupor.

"Yes. It can be booked for tours," the old man said, keeping his gaze on the far end of the strip. "But that man will be gone for three days."

"Three days? What kind of tour is that?" the Sicilian asked.

"Not a tour. The passenger was going to Luena in Angola. He said he might be gone for three days."

"There must be interesting things to see in Luena, to go for three days."

The aged African's face changed only in that his eyebrows lifted slightly. "I don't know. I have never been to Luena." He paused, then added, "It has an airport. And a road that goes to the sea. And a railroad. I think there is a railroad."

"I would like to go to Luena when the pilot returns," the Sicilian said. "How can I reserve the helicopter?"

"There is a card on the board inside," the man said without moving. "You book through Upper Zambezi Tours."

"Thank you. I will give them a call. How will I know when the helicopter is returning."

"They will call you. Where will you be?"

"The River Horse Lodge. Do I need anything to go to Luena?"

"You will need a visa."

"How do I get one?"

"I can get you one." The old man still didn't move. The Sicilian stood beside the bench until the gray head turned and looked up at him. "When you come for your flight," he said. "I will get your visa then. It will cost two hundred dollars."

Much to the confusion of the Kellermans, the man who called himself Eraldo Manco had remained in his cottage at the River Horse Lodge during the entire two day wait, having meals delivered to his room, and spending daylight hours on his small balcony watching animals come to the river. On the third morning, he checked out of the lodge shortly after the dawn safaris ventured into the bush.

The flight operations building was shuttered up tight when he arrived, but he was a man who was accustomed to being patient. He dismissed his driver and planted himself on the rough-cut bench, watching baboons chase each other across the abandoned field in the morning haze. The call from the tour company notifying him that the helicopter was on its way back from Luena reached him just before 9:00 a.m. The old man who could get him a visa did not arrive until an hour later. He was standing beside the building's single desk, watching the ancient manager laboriously transfer his passport information to an equally seasoned computer when Marshall Pollard called. And he was again sitting on the wooden bench, waiting for his flight, when the pilot called to say he had discovered the Kodiak. His patience had been rewarded. The day was going to be much more productive than he had possibly anticipated.

17

Taylor refused to stop for lunch. She trudged along the naked stretch of riverbank as if she were Atlas with the weight of the world crushing her shoulders. She now carried only the small pack with her precious bones. Matt walked three steps behind, struggling to maintain a slow enough pace to keep from tripping on her heels. When he approached too close, a sharp rebuke, chained to a string of complaints, reminded him he was neglecting his responsibilities.

"Stay back there and keep an eye on those ugly dogs," she snapped. "Why don't they leave us alone? I'm not stopping for one of those nasty bag-cooked lunches while they're back there. That thing they call a beef taco is one of the grossest things I've ever eaten. How do they get army people to eat that shit anyway?"

Matt turned to check the progress of the hyenas, thinking for the hundredth time that he should tell her they were more closely related to cats than dogs. But it was one of those useless bits of trivia that would illicit a "So, who gives a damn? They look like dogs to me" response that wasn't worth adding to her list of gripes.

The floodplain was wide here, and the four animals stayed on the higher bank where they could move through the scrub with some cover. He had first seen them an hour after they broke camp, trotting along in a small pack until almost even with them, then sitting silently in the shade of a thicket until their prey was a hundred yards ahead. They stalked in complete silence, with none of the growls, snarls, and giddy laughter with which they had tortured the couple during the night.

He didn't argue with Taylor about a stop. The hyenas were unnerving, and he wasn't certain how they would react if their quarry paused or sat for any length of time. He had pulled packages of what passed for trail mix from two of the ration packets, and they ate as they moved. When he did stop long enough to scoop out a filtering hole and refill their water bottles beside what was now a shallow, murky stream, Taylor continued to walk around him in a tight circle, proving to the scavengers that they were still mobile and very much alive.

"When we see some acacias that are close to the bank and haven't been trimmed too high, we'll stop and make a boma," he called to her. "I think I need to shoot a couple of those things and let them either eat each other or decide it's not worth hanging around. I've been told they'll attack wounded members of their own packs, and that might give them what they want. We'll just have to hope it doesn't draw any of the big cats."

"What am I supposed to do while you chop up the tree and make a ring?" she called back.

"I don't give a damn. Walk in a circle again. Hide behind the tree. Climb the damn thing if you want. Hyenas can't climb."

"Yeah. Like I'm going to climb up one of these thorny trees," she yelled over her shoulder.

He quickened his step to get to within civil conversation distance. "I'll get some limbs down to make a barrier until we can shape the ring. You just keep it between you and the hyenas."

"All the trees are over on the bank where the dogs are," she complained. "How are we supposed to get to one without getting closer?"

"We'll just have to count on them giving us some space," he said. "When we see the right trees, I might drop one and let them work on the dead animal while we build a shelter." She didn't reply and slouched heavily forward for another hour before reaching a stretch where the steeper bank moved in toward what was left of the river.

"There are a couple over there," she called back to him. Matt had seen the umbrella-shaped trees but was hoping for another mile or two before giving in to her. He decided it wasn't worth another half hour of complaints.

"Head over that way. When we get closer to the bank, I'll . . ." He was interrupted in mid-sentence by the appearance on the top of the embankment of another of Africa's creatures that looked as if it had been cobbled together by some malevolent god using leftover pieces. Its long, sloping face was a streak of black against heavy striped shoulders that fell away to narrow hips. A dozen of the wildebeests paused at the edge of the steep drop, watched the two creatures that were unfamiliar to them through small, curious eyes, and decided they were harmless enough that they shouldn't keep them from water. The hyenas had also seen the powerful horned animals and dropped out of sight into a tall patch of dry grass.

"We're in luck," Matt muttered, causing Taylor to stop and turn. He nodded toward the animals that were now sliding awkwardly down the bank and moving toward the river at a wary trot. "Those are favorites of hyenas. I think your dogs would give us up in a minute for a night feasting on one of them. The hyenas saw them, and I think are watching them now instead of us. When we get over by the bank, I'll bring one down and let the beasts work on it while we build our boma."

The plan gave Taylor purpose. Her step quickened, and she beat Matt to the base of the embankment where she stopped, looked back at the drinking herd, and cocked her head impatiently. He lowered his pack, swung the rifle from his shoulder, and dropped to one knee. The shot was long, probably a hundred yards, but one of the young bulls stood broadside to him. He caught the animal directly behind the front shoulder, toppling it sideways onto the water's edge.

Taylor released a muffled squeal as the herd bolted, some galloping wildly downstream, the others dashing back toward the bush. The hyenas, startled by the sharp report of the rifle, seemed to sense what had happened and didn't give chase. They remained crouched in the grass, eying the fallen bull.

Matt pushed Taylor ahead of him up the bank and followed her to the closest of the thorny trees that was large enough to yield the branches they needed. While he hacked at the lower limbs, she watched the pack of scavengers.

"They're going down there," she murmured under her breath. "It worked."

Matt stacked the cuttings, systematically circling them with a barrier laced with needle-sharp spears. "That bull should keep them busy for a while. I hope it's long enough for us to get through the night and away from here tomorrow before they decide we're still interesting."

"I wouldn't think the four could eat that whole thing that fast," she said.

Matt snorted. "Watch them. By the time it gets dark, most of it will be gone. I wish I'd shot two."

From behind the screen of spiked branches, Taylor watched in horror as the hunched beasts tore at the dead animal, growling and snapping at each other as if each wanted the kill to itself. She turned away with a shiver, making a slow, deliberate turn to survey their surroundings over the top of the boma.

"I don't like being up here in the middle of all these . . ." She stopped in mid-sentence and squinted into the glare of the late afternoon sun. "What's that over there?" she whispered, pointing toward two taller, upright trees that branched high above the ground fifty feet farther into the bush. Matt followed her extended finger. A dun-colored bundle hung loosely over a limb twenty feet above the bare circle of clay that surrounded the tree.

"Shit," he muttered.

"What's wrong? What is it?"

"It's a duiker or some other kind of antelope."

Taylor stared at him in disbelief. "How did it get caught up in that tree?"

"It was put there," he said grimly. "By a leopard. And it will be coming back for it tonight."

18

For a man who spent a good part of every day reviewing reports and studying maps, Adam considered himself to be in pretty decent shape. He and Dreu both worked from standing desks for at least part of each day, and their daily routine included either a five-mile morning jog or an hour on their mountain bikes in the national forest north of Scottsdale. But this Yander was a beast. The man ran barefoot over ground that poked at Adam's soles through his boots. He guessed the African's calloused feet must be at least as tough as whatever made up the bottoms of Adam's low, flexible hikers. And Yander's toes gave the agile little man better traction where the sand was soft. Adam seemed to lose half a step for every one he took forward. The big American's only salvation was a longer stride and the tracker's intuitive sense that he needed to stop to study a print or crushed tuft of grass whenever his client was about to shout for a break. And he consciously waited an extra few minutes before falling again into his steady, loping gait.

They found what Yander called a boma where the couple had camped and slept. And just before sundown, another. Yander crouched intently around the inside of the second ring, then announced that it had been the couple's shelter the night before.

"We will stay here tonight," he said, dropping his thin bedroll inside the circle. "We will find them tomorrow. Gather wood. I will find something to eat."

Their meals to that point had been a strong spicy jerky and slices of what Adam guessed to be dried plantain. Until now, Yander had not stopped for meals, chewing constantly at the dried meat as he ran. He refilled their water bottles when he found one of the shallow wells dug by the fugitives, then drank in stride.

"Your friend knows something about living in the bush," he remarked as he returned to their night's shelter carrying a two-foot monitor lizard. "He digs those holes to keep the river worms out of his water. And he builds a good boma."

"He's a man who has had to survive by his wits for a long time," Adam acknowledged, drawing an inquiring look from his guide. Adam turned the conversation to the lizard. "How did you catch that thing? I didn't hear a shot."

Yander grinned, holding the reptile high by its tail. "He hid in a place that trapped him. I hope your friend does not do the same. He is being followed."

"Followed? By someone who's ahead of us?"

"By the four hyenas."

"Can you tell if he knows?"

The tracker shrugged. "If he is observant, he knows. They are not always staying back in the bush." Yander forced a long spit through the lizard and prepared a fire. "Tonight, we will eat better," he announced, his grin widening. "As you Americans like to say, these taste like chicken."

Adam glanced casually about. "While you cook that thing up, I need to make a private call." He held up his satellite phone. "Will I be safer down by the river, or back in the bush?"

The tracker's grin didn't waver. "I would go out in the space between. Then, if anything comes for you, you will at least see it before it gets to you. And we can both try to shoot it."

Small comfort, Adam thought, and forced aside enough of the boughs with their two-inch barbs to climb from the boma. He found a position midway between the steep bank and the river's edge where he could be seen by the African and had an open view in every direction. Dreu took a moment to get to the phone.

"Did I get you up?" he asked jokingly.

"Up from a message intercept that should worry you," she said seriously. "I've been following all the internal messages that include key words that might relate to your search, the two Agency guys that are following you, or your part of Africa. Your timing is perfect. Where are you?"

"Somewhere in the bush between Zambezi in Zambia and Kuito in Angola. Can't you get a fix on the phone?"

"I'm not where I can try," she said with a trace of irritation. "But the Agency men—this Pollard and Turnley—are right behind you. They reported that they're in Zambezi waiting for a way to get into Angola tomorrow. Some place called Luena."

"That might still put them two days back," Adam guessed. "Is that what was worrying you?"

"No. Much worse. In the contact they made with Langley today, this Pollard asked to speak to the director personally. He has some Langley experience and is concerned that someone is ahead of them on this search who seems to have better information than he has. His question to the director was about whether there was any truth to the rumors that had been around for years about a group called Unit One. He suggested that the Unit—if it exists—might have an interest in getting to Page."

Adam was silent long enough that she checked to make sure she hadn't lost the connection.

"Yes. I'm here," he murmured. "I'm just thinking about what this means. What did the director say?"

"He gave him a Washington-type answer. Said he wasn't aware of anyone else who might want to find Page."

"But didn't say anything about the Unit, one way or the other?"

"No. A non-answer to that part of the question. But here's what worries me more. After the call, he immediately shot off a request that Page's background information be re-examined. He asked that they look for past acquaintances that had been brought into the Agency or who essentially disappeared over the years. I think you might show up."

"If I do, they'll have a hard time figuring out what happened to me. I have no records anywhere."

"That's just it. Page will have Air Force records, and they will include his connection to your fabled landing. But then, Tom Mercomes disappears. They'll find some old pictures of you and create images with what they think a surgically-altered face might look like. And they'll know they can look for a man with a prosthetic eye. If they work hard enough at it, Adam, they will find you passing through airports on your way to Lusaka. Phipps will confirm that you were the man who came to see him, impersonating an NSA officer."

"Why would he want to go to all that trouble based on a shot-in-the-dark question by an African head-of-station?"

Dreu's voice became edgy. "Oh, come on, Adam. This guy has never liked having us out here. He's tolerated us partly because he isn't sure how to shut us down and partly because every now and then we do something important for him. He likes control, and he doesn't have it where the Unit is concerned. I think he was about to try to talk the president into closing us down when we got in the way of the Marburg buy. The rescue of the Panchen Lama was big for the president and bought us time. But if he thinks you're interfering with them finding Page, he'll come after us."

This time she didn't interrupt Adam's silence, knowing that he was still there, but processing. He was turning in a slow circle, wondering whether his greatest danger now lurked beneath the dark surface of the river, crouched in the shadowy bush along the upper bank, or waited for morning transportation that would bring them closer to a rendezvous that might confirm the existence of Unit 1.

19

Pollard disconnected the call and scowled at Turnley. They sat across from each other at a round, ebony-topped table, each nursing a cup of black coffee and nibbling at a day-old sweet roll. They had refused to bribe the old man who passed for airfield manager in Zambezi to give them a pass on advanced reservations in Angola. Pollard's search for a hotel in Luena that would meet his inflexible visa requirement had turned up only one: a three-star accommodation cryptically called the "iu" Hotel. Much to their surprise, the place had turned out to be clean and comfortable with its own bar and restaurant, private baths and an adequate, but uninspiring buffet.

"I take it you didn't learn much," Turnley guessed, dipping a turn of his roll in his coffee.

"He was at least willing to take the call," Pollard said. "They're nervous about Page suddenly showing up and are afraid that if he's found, he'll go public. As you could hear, he wanted to know what progress we've made. He was especially interested to know that the plane has shown up, and that it's in Angola."

Turnley gave a quick nod. "But he wasn't willing to offer any explanation about how someone might already have known where it was and be a few days ahead of us." It was a statement rather than a question.

Pollard stared through the sheers on the window beside them at the pink square office building that was their only view of the city of Luena. "His answer was no answer," he muttered. "When I asked specifically if there was such a thing as Unit One and if they might have someone interested in Page, he just said I'd been listening to too much talk around the water cooler when I was at

Langley." He turned and smiled cynically at his partner. "Then he asked that if we came across anyone who might be this 'party of interest,' we get some photos and shoot them back to HQ. So he's wondering what the hell's going on as well."

Turnley glanced about at the four other patrons scattered about the dining room: a middle-aged couple and two businessmen in white shirts and ties. All African. The Italian, whose ride they had hijacked from Zambezi, had not registered with them, but had waited at the airport for a domestic flight to Huambo.

"What did you make of the tour pilot's story?" Turnley asked. "When he took us to see the plane, it seemed to me like he hovered a little longer over the site than he needed to before landing. Almost like he was blowing away any evidence that he'd put down there before, possibly with someone with him."

Pollard's cynicism deepened. "It did the job. I didn't see prints anywhere close to the plane. And when we went farther out, there were only the man's and the woman's. But it's quite a coincidence that he supposedly flew this Mr. Solomon over here, checked into the hotel without him, and happened to get a tip from another pilot that there might be a plane on the ground in the bush. He says Solomon left him at the airport, and he doesn't know what happened to him."

"So—what's your theory?"

Pollard frowned into his coffee. "Whoever this guy is took Nelson . . . wasn't that his name? Nelson? Anyway, he took Nelson by the plane on the way here. Same route we took. Solomon didn't stay here and didn't take either of the flights out of here to Luanda or Huambo. And he didn't charter a plane. So he got a ride of some kind and went overland. The question is where?"

"One of a *lot* of questions," Turnley corrected. "I'm wondering how Solomon knew where the plane was? Is he in touch with Page and the woman, or does he have some pretty good intel that found the thing for him when, from what you could tell, the director didn't know it was there? And why let Nelson 'make the discovery?' Why not just keep the plane's location secret and keep on tracking Page?"

"My guess is to keep us sitting in Zambezi for an extra day," Pollard ventured. "If Solomon had come directly here and just been dropped off, why would Nelson stay overnight? He's based out of Zambia, said he didn't know anyone here, and didn't look like a guy who would spend money to stay over if he didn't need to. Unless there was some incentive to take an extra day getting back."

Turnley nodded thoughtfully. "Like the reward for discovering the missing plane."

"Exactly. It looks like the man will get it. And what that suggests to me is that this Solomon knows we're behind him and was willing to trade off the plane for an extra day. That all brings us back to some pretty good intelligence on his part. I don't think he's in touch with Page. He's trying to find him. But he has a pretty good idea where to look."

"When we asked Nelson where someone would go if they hiked out from the plane, he thought they would head upriver, take the first road they came to, and get a ride here to Luena. But there's no record of them staying here. And these are the only digs in town. The local police don't seem to know anything about other westerners in town. And this is a small place."

Pollard sniffed cynically. "They wouldn't have reported in. In fact, they'd keep their heads low and probably bribe someone to keep moving them west. Toward Kuito."

"That's 400 kilometers. Probably five hours by car. Do you want to skip the hotel and go tonight?"

Pollard glanced out the window again at the waning daylight. "I'll call for a charter for early tomorrow morning," he said. "There's nothing we could do in Kuito tonight that we can't do then. But I think I will get in touch with our Angola people and see if they can get us some police help. We need to check every hotel in the city to see what foreigners have been in town the last few days."

20

Neither of the American CIA men had been at all hesitant about discussing their search for Nicholas Page with the Sicilian sitting in a seat a few feet behind them in the helicopter. He had introduced himself as Eraldo Manco, an agent with a travel group out of Naples that sought out exotic, out-of-the-way adventure tours for the eco-tourist set. He had been in Zambezi to check out the Water Horse Lodge and upper stretches of the river, away from Victoria Falls and the high density tourist areas. Next stop, the national parks in western Angola.

"The country is just coming back from its civil war," he explained, "and the parks are still largely undiscovered. Beautiful and empty. Ideal for those who want that 'off the beaten track' adventure."

He had agreed immediately to the diversion to the downed plane and listened without comment as the men theorized about why the Kodiak had taken that particular route and why it had gone down.

"It looks to me like he was making a beeline for Benguela or Sumbe on the coast," Pollard had conjectured. "Or maybe to refuel in Huambo."

"Why west instead of east?" Turnley wondered aloud. "The other coast was a lot closer."

"Exactly," Pollard said. "If he hadn't crashed, they would have reached the Angolan coast within a day. They could have been out of the country while everyone was still waiting for them to come back from their little supply run to Mozambique. A pretty clever plan if he hadn't gone down."

"Assuming this is his plane . . ."

"From Nelson's description, I'd say it's a pretty sure thing,"

Pollard replied. "Just the fact that someone tried to cover it suggests it wasn't a lost tourist plane. In that case, people would be out waving their shirts around a big bonfire."

Once on the ground beside the river, the Sicilian had waited beside the helicopter while the Americans did an initial search. As they clambered about inside the fuselage, he had checked their position on one of Nelson's charts, seen the sets of prints heading west, and noted that there were only two. Solomon hadn't been dropped here, but may have been taken further upriver. Possibly to meet the couple. Possibly to fall in somewhere behind them. The Italian returned to the chart and tried to project where the fugitives were headed.

If I were Page, he thought, *I would stay with the river as long as I could, then continue to avoid towns and villages until I reached a place where two or three whites could blend with the safari crowds without drawing attention. That would not be Luena. Possibly Kuito. But ideally Huambo. But what then?*

He agreed with Pollard that Page had gone west because it was the route no one would expect. Would he do the same when he reached whatever city he chose? Continue to the coast, or go north or south into one of the bordering countries? To guess wrong could put the Sicilian out of position when Page finally surfaced. The safe move was to hole up in a place where he could move quickly in any direction and hope Magnum44 could keep him ahead of the two station chiefs.

When the agents completed their examination of the plane's interior, he feigned natural curiosity and asked to have a look himself. No one objected. The cockpit yielded no clues. There were no signs of injury, and Page had taken any charts that might be useful. What he failed to find in the rear of the plane did pique his curiosity. No fire extinguisher. No standard life vests. The chopper pilot, he guessed, knew more about this downed plane than he was telling his passengers.

21

Just before the sun reached its zenith, they heard the shot. Distant, but distinct. Yander was trotting five paces ahead of Adam and, within two strides, stopped dead still. He tilted his head like a jackal testing the breeze and waited. There was no second report.

"I think your friend is in trouble," the tracker said without turning. "He would not be shooting game this early in the day, and they should be farther ahead of us."

Adam stopped beside him. "It may not be them. Possibly hunters."

Yander shook his head dismissively. "Not here. This is not good for hunting. From the old diamond mine to the road to Kuito, many of the animals were killed during the war. Guides do not bring hunters here."

Adam's thoughts flew to the conversation with Dreu. Had the Agency men somehow bypassed them and found Matt? And if they had, would he shoot at them or they at him? His fear was that out in this isolated bush country, either was possible.

"We need to move up onto the upper bank," Yander said. "I would like to see what is causing this trouble before it sees us." He broke again into his loping trot, but steered them toward the steep, head-high slope that separated the brushy land of the plateau from the open riverbed. After what seemed to Adam to be another kilometer, the African slowed to a cautious crouch and held up a quieting hand. Ahead, out of sight above them, they heard the growls and snarls of fighting animals.

"Hyenas," Yander whispered. "They have either attacked your friend, or he shot one and they have attacked it." He turned back to a spot where brush didn't crowd the edge of the upper tier and scrambled up the bank with Adam close behind. They continued away from the floodplain until the sound of quarreling animals was well off to their right, then circled again west, turning back toward the ungodly shrieks and gnashing when the fracas was directly between them and the river. As they approached a thicket of low, grey-leafed brush, Yander waved Adam to a stop, eased to the edge of the clump, and dropped to one knee. In rapid succession he fired two shots, then followed a fleeing animal in his sights until it disappeared into the bush. He remained crouched for a moment, staring in the direction of his targets, then gestured for Adam to join him.

Fifty yards ahead two hyenas, one still quivering in its death throes, lay beside the ravaged remains of a third. Yander stood, and the men approached the fallen animals, the guide warily scanning the bush around them. As they neared the open patch of blood-stained ground, Adam saw movement behind a chest-high wall of acacia thorns to their left. Nick rose slowly in the center of the boma, warily watching the two armed men, his own rifle hanging at the ready.

"You having a little trouble there, Page?" Adam called, grinning broadly. The man looked at him as if he knew the voice, but the face didn't match.

"Yeah, it's me," Adam said. "Cyclops. I've had a little work done since you saw me last, but it's me."

The man squinted over the top of the wall of thorns, canting his head to one side. "*Well, I'll be damned,*" he shouted. "What the hell are you doing here?"

Adam cast an exaggerated look at the pile of dead hyenas. "We heard you were having trouble with some of the locals. Came to clean up the neighborhood."

A blonde head raised above the thorn barrier beside Matt, the woman's hair pulled back into a short, loose ponytail. Even after a week in the bush, the unembellished face was prettier than Taylor Dennis had appeared in the pictures Adam had seen. Intense blue eyes over a pert nose and full lips. A sun-bronzed complexion that accentuated her light eyes. She stared suspiciously at Yander, then fixed her gaze on Adam.

"You know this man?" she asked her partner.

Nick laughed and let the arm with the rifle relax. "Know him? Hell, this guy is the closest thing to a brother I've ever had. He owes me his life!"

Adam's wrinkled brow sent a message that his old friend shouldn't say more. He and Yander skirted the boma to the side away from the dead animals while Nick used the butt of his rifle to force an opening along the base of the acacia tree. His old wingman drew Adam into a long, grunting embrace, then pushed him back to arms-length while he ran a critical eye over his friend's new face. "*Hmph!*" was all he said, then turned to inspect the African tracker. "Glad to see the two of you. How the hell did you find us?"

Adam looked quickly at Taylor who was clearly interested in hearing the answer. "Well, you two have drawn a lot of international attention," he said, then added cryptically to Nick, "And you've appeared back on the radar."

Nick's face tightened. "And how do you happen to know this?"

"Let's just say I'm in a position to be able to monitor this kind of thing."

"Do we have incoming?" Nick asked, falling back on Air Force jargon.

"There are bogies at your six," Adam said. "We need to get you two out of here. We can talk as we go."

"How did you get here? Where's your transportation?" the woman asked.

Yander flashed her a wide smile. "We walked. Just like you have walked—but a little faster. Now we will all walk together."

"*You walked?*" The question was half snarl, half sob. "You mean, I have to keep hiking in this damn heat? I hope you have something better to eat than the shit he had with him."

105

"MRE's," Nick explained with an eye roll that told Adam all he needed to know. Yander's smile became an amused laugh. He pulled a finger-length of charred meat from the leather pouch on his waist and handed it to Taylor. "I saved this for you. It is from the back of the lizard. Tastes just like chicken."

She turned aside in disgust. "You're joking, right? You couldn't have just hiked here to find us. There's a road or something nearby."

"There is a road," Yander acknowledged, nodding upstream. "We are near the beginning of the river. Just beyond there, maybe half a day if we move quickly, we will come to a road. It can take us up to Cuemba. Not very far. Maybe another six hours."

"Oh, God," Taylor exclaimed. "You *weren't* joking!"

"Cuemba?" Nick asked. "How far is that from Kuito?"

Yander shrugged. "Maybe one hundred fifty kilometers. Maybe more."

"Shit," Nick muttered, turning to Adam. "We're trying to stay out of sight, for reasons you just described. I was hoping we were closer to Kuito."

"We can figure this out as we go," Adam said, glancing again over the thorn barrier at the heap of dead animals. "Why didn't you shoot the rest of the damn things yourself?"

Nick waited for Taylor to throw her pack over her shoulder and pushed her reluctantly through the opening in the boma, then waited for Yander and Adam to follow. He stepped up beside his friend as they headed toward the scarp that descended to what was left of the river.

"We had one hell of a night," he muttered, throwing a nod back over his shoulder. "See that tree back there with what's left of an antelope hanging in it? A leopard sat up there half the night crunching on that thing, while the hyenas paced back and forth and yapped at us." He pointed at a purple stain beside the stream ahead of them. "I shot a pretty good-sized wildebeest to get the hyenas working on something other than us. The four of them ate the whole thing in a couple of hours—horns and all. Then the vultures picked the ground clean. The hyena's bellies were hanging like they had bloat, but I guess they never feel like they've had enough. They decided we looked like an easy breakfast and camped out where you found them. When the leopard finally left, I shot the hyena you saw, hoping we could get out of here and leave them behind while they ate up their buddy. They stayed interested enough in us that we didn't dare leave." He patted the butt of the rifle that hung across his back. "With that leopard still hanging around and no clear idea how much farther we had to go, I hated to keep using ammunition."

"Sounds like we showed up at just the right time," Adam said with a chuckle.

"Damn right! And I'm still interested to know how you found us."

"And I am interested in how you suddenly became Nick," a female voice called back to them.

Yander kept them moving until they reached what he called "the road to Cuemba," a set of tracks pressed into the hardpack of the Angolan plateau that was barely distinguishable from the harsh landscape around it.

"Does anyone ever come down here?" Adam asked, kicking at an undisturbed clump of grass in one of the ruts.

Yander turned and looked south along the path. "Not often. There was once a mine in that direction. Sometimes hunters use it. But, as I told you, this is not a good place to hunt. We will have to walk to Cuemba."

As the tracker helped Nick cut branches in the dwindling light for a larger boma, Adam gathered wood and shaped the boughs into a protective circle around a sulking Taylor.

"Some rescuers you are," she pouted, hunching over a heating bag of chili. "Now, instead of one, I'm stuck out here with three guys who all think they're Indiana Jones."

Adam threw a thorn-covered limb onto the growing pile, a two-inch needle catching his wrist and leaving a long red welt across the side of his arm and hand. "Damn!" he muttered under his breath. "These things are like razor wire!"

"Up till now," Taylor grumbled, "they've kept everything out we wanted kept out."

He scowled at her over the tangled barrier. "You sound like you're not too excited about having been found."

"We weren't supposed to be here in the first place."

"But here you are."

"No thanks to him," she scoffed, casting Nick a disgusted nod of the head.

"Thanks to him, you're alive." Adam countered, licking a thin line of blood from his wrist. "And not in a Zambian jail. So you might be grateful for that."

"Thanks to him, I'm not in Luanda. I was supposed to be there a week ago."

Adam more carefully tossed another limb onto the boma wall. "I didn't realize you were headed for Luanda. Your course was taking you to Benguela."

"Yeah. Well, whatever," she retorted. "And why do you call him Nick?"

"That's what I knew him by when we worked together," Adam said, feeling no need to explain further.

"Yeah, well, I think he hasn't been telling me everything," she grumbled.

"I can't imagine that," Adam muttered and went in search of more firewood.

With the boma complete, a fire burning, and Yander roasting a guinea fowl over the flames, Adam drew Nick out onto the open swath left by the old mining road, far enough from the boma not to be overheard.

"The Agency ID'd you from a picture posted in one of the newspapers about the lost plane," he told his old flying partner.

"They have at least two people trying to locate you and, probably because of me, they know you came into Angola."

Nick studied him suspiciously. "First of all, tell me what you're doing here and how you found me. Then you can fill me in on why that brought two Agency men in this direction."

Adam shook his head soberly. "I can't tell you everything—just that I'm in a position that gives me access to what's going on inside the Agency. You've been in that position, so you know what I mean. We—me and my partner—saw some internal memos that alerted the people in Clandestine Ops that Nick Page had surfaced, identified as the missing Matt Hylton. I saw the photo, knew it was you, and knew they were coming after you. I couldn't very well let them get to you before I could find you and help you stay out of sight. That's what I'm doing here." He grinned at his old wingman in the dim light of the distant fire.

"As for how I found you, I tried to think like Nick Page. Don't go where you said you were going. Head for a coast where you have a number of escape options. Take a route that doesn't seem possible, given what you were flying. I checked the max range on the Kodiak and saw that you could barely reach Benguela if you flew low, kept the speed down, and had a favoring tailwind. My associate was able to scan that route using comparative satellite images and located the plane."

Nick arched an impressed brow. "That's a pretty capable associate." He paused, frowning darkly at Adam. "So—you must have also sold your soul to the company store."

"Not exactly," was all Adam would say. "And yes, I have a very capable partner. The problem for us now is that, along the way, I had to question the professor at the dig site in Kabwe. The CIA guys had been there already and were checking places going east where you might have hidden a plane. When they came up empty, they went back to Dr. Phipps and learned I'd been there poking around. It wasn't hard for them to learn I'd flown to Zambezi and chartered a helicopter. They talked to the pilot, found the Kodiak, and the last I heard, were in Luena. My guess is they've got people watching every town between there and the coast."

"Shit," Nick muttered under his breath, gazing back grimly at the two figures crouched inside the ring of thorns. "I was hoping we could safely turn up in Kuito and get a ride to Benguela without drawing too much attention."

Adam shook his head. "I don't think so. But you're not trying to get to Luanda?"

Nick cocked his head. "Luanda? Hell, no. I got a couple of berths on a cargo ship leaving Benguela a week from now for Panama. The ship won't even be in port for another four days."

"A week from now?" Adam squinted through the flickering shadows cast by the fire. "Why so late?"

Nick grinned back at him. "I had to learn some things along the way. Plus, I figured we'd be better off to disappear completely for a couple of weeks and let the search die down."

Adam looked again toward the boma and the slim figure of Taylor Dennis who now stood, watching the men in the distant shadows. "Did you learn what you needed to know?" he asked.

Nick's frown showed both disappointment and embarrassment. "I'm afraid I did," he muttered.

Adam nodded thoughtfully. "If I'd cleared off that Kodiak, pulled it out of the wash, and hotwired the starter, could I have flown it out of there?"

Nick shrugged. "I don't think I did much damage to it."

"What did you tell her was wrong?"

"Loss of oil pressure and torque."

"And she couldn't see that the oil pressure was staying up?"

"She had no idea where to look."

"Hmmm," Adam muttered. "That's a pretty risky way to learn what kind of woman you're with—and whether she's that committed to you."

Nick shrugged. "I knew we could make it out. And I had a feeling it was about time for me to change residences anyway. I knew that if I took this woman, I was taking one hell of a risk." His face tightened into a thin smile. "You know, Cyclops, that I've never been much with the ladies. This face is one even a mother has trouble loving. So when Taylor seemed to be able to get past all the scars and how damn awkward I get, I admit I was pretty well taken in. I knew how desperately I wanted her love to be real, but I also knew she needed my help to get her out with those damn bones. I had to be sure one was as real as the other." He turned and followed Adam's gaze toward the fire. "I learned pretty fast that it wasn't."

Adam was silent for a long moment, struggling to find the right thing to say. He finally took two steps farther back into the shadows and pulled out his satphone. "Give me a minute here," he said. "I need to check in with the boss."

He could tell from Dreu's breathing that he'd caught her during her morning run. "I've been waiting to hear from you," she said breathlessly. "Something's going on you need to know about."

"First of all," Adam cut in, "I've found Nick. He's right here with me, so be aware of that as we talk. Now, what's happened?"

"The Agency's gone silent," she said, her breath gradually slowing. "Not a word about you or this search. I think there must be some internal instruction that all communication must be by written memo, hand delivered. They know we have access to all electronic exchanges, so they've shut us off."

"Even calls coming in from outside? From Pollard and Turnley?"

"I think they must have set up some kind of separate link that's independent of the normal coded systems. I picked up a call yesterday, and nothing since. But that one worries me."

Adam turned his back to Nick and the fire flickering through the ring of thorns. "What did it say?"

"The director told Pollard that if they got close enough to this Mr. Solomon to get a photo and send it back to Langley for analysis. I think the director suspects you're with the Unit, and he wants to discover who you are."

Adam sniffed in disgust into the phone. "You were right. I've created an exposure that could be costly. Now, I've just got to figure out how to get us out of this without doing more damage."

"Well, be very careful," Dreu said anxiously. "I can't give you good information about what they're up to." She paused, then added, "but there's one other thing that might be helpful. You know I mentioned that Taylor Dennis has a close male friend at the university who took off a week ago for parts unknown?"

Adam grunted an acknowledgement, looking back at Nick who was consciously trying to appear disinterested.

"Well, our Wesley Epling wasn't that hard to follow. He's been systematically making his way to Africa. More specifically, to the Angolan capital. Luanda."

"From what I just learned, that doesn't surprise me," he answered. "And I don't think it will surprise Nick. And that reminds me. Do you still have access to Agency files?"

He heard Dreu chuckle. "They're a long way from figuring out how we get into the system," she said. "What do you need?"

Adam lowered his voice to a soft whisper. "See if you can find anyone else who might have reason to want to find Nick. I ran into a character flying to Zambezi who said he was going there to hunt an antelope that's almost extinct. The helicopter pilot told me the few that still remain are hundreds of miles from there. The guy's story—and the timing—seemed pretty suspicious."

"I'll see what I can find. You might ask Nick."

"I will. But I want to get us away from this Dennis woman first. She's toxic."

22

Turnley took up residence in a hotel in Kuito that was a carbon copy of the one the Agency men had occupied in Luena. After a quick refueling, Pollard took the chartered plane on to Benguela to begin searching departures from coastal ports and airfields and check out Anglo visitors to the port.

Though a city of nearly half a million, Kuito had only four hotels with amenities that might reasonably attract western visitors. With the help of a local policeman, Turnley was able to visit each during the first morning, checking registration logs for the previous week and interviewing the few non-African patrons. All were European and all, but one, engineers in the city to assist with rebuilding the rail line that had once connected eastern cities to the coast. The single non-engineer, a representative of the government of Portugal, administered a grant for general refurbishing of the city center after the devastation of ten years of siege by warring military factions.

In the afternoon, Turnley combed outlying areas with the local officer, stopping unannounced at every place the policeman knew there might be a room for let. After two stops, the CIA man knew that, from what he had learned about the mercurial Taylor Dennis from her colleagues at the dig site, the woman would not have tolerated any of them: dingy, bug-infested, without running water, and featuring open-trench outhouses in the rear that were no more than rough boards stretched over pools of raw sewage.

Away from the main thoroughfare, where every building glistened with a new coat of pink stucco, the city still showed the ravages of war. Bullet-riddled walls stood untouched. What had once been an apartment building now resembled a stack of broken concrete boxes. The agent returned to the hotel and booked a car and driver to take him to Benguela. He would run similar checks at towns of any size on the way to the coast, but doubted he would find his fugitives.

Pollard had just settled into a quiet interior room overlooking a manicured garden courtyard at Benguela's Hotel Residential when a call from the director redirected their plans.

"Get up to Luanda," his boss instructed. "We've been backgrounding the Dennis woman and learned that she has a male friend who left town about the time she and Page disappeared. The name's Epling. Wesley Epling. He's now at the Hotel Continental in the capital. My guess is that if you keep an eye on him, the woman and Page will come to him."

Pollard called Turnley, suggested he catch a flight at Huambo to the capital, and meet him at the Hotel Continental. "If we can get there before the woman does," he told his partner, "I think we're going to catch the sonofabitch."

23

The encrypted message from Magnum44 to the man from Taormina gave the Sicilian the same information.

University colleague of Taylor Dennis (and fiancé) Wesley Epling has flown to Luanda. Checked into Hotel Continental. May be awaiting a rendezvous there. Her location and Page's still unknown.

He read it carefully, made a mental note of *Hotel Continental* and *Wesley Epling*, then permanently deleted the text. He had been sitting on the balcony of his room in Huambo with feet propped on the railing, studying a map of Southern Africa on which he had drawn a line from Kabwe in Zambia through the site where the plane had been found, and on to the Angolan coast. The line extended right through where he now sat and ended in Benguela, 250 miles south of Epling and the Hotel Continental. He leaned back, head tilted skyward and eyes closed, and again tried to insert himself into the devious mind of Nicholas Page.

He was confident the man had not been headed for Luanda. Page didn't have the fuel to stay that far south, then divert when deeper into Angola. He had been planning to land in Benguela or the nearby port of Lobito. Was Epling expecting to meet them there after they arrived? The Sicilian had a strong suspicion that Taylor Dennis had other plans.

Pollard and Turnley had intimated that Page and this Dennis woman were in some kind of relationship, one that was close enough to convince Page to be an accessory to her theft. This whole adventure didn't seem to the Sicilian like the actions of a man who knew he was flying his lover to meet a fiancé. It smacked of a seductive anthropologist planning to ditch her chump of an inamorato and make her way solo to Luanda. Would Page have fallen for something like that? From what he remembered of the homely, often awkward man from their Syrian days, he suspected he would. The thought of Page being jilted brought a curled smile to the Italian's lips.

But now, Page and the woman were still out there in the bush somewhere, trying to survive and reach a place of safety. If they made it, what would she do? The Sicilian was certain she knew her fiancé was waiting for her. He was almost as certain she would get rid of Page and try to hook up with Epling. And once that happened, he didn't give a damn about Taylor Dennis. He wanted to know where Nick Page would go. And the best way to learn that was to stay put near the center of the action until he heard again from Magnum. And Huambo was just the spot.

24

During her short year with the CIA, Amanda Nguyen had met the director only once, the month she joined the agency at a dinner welcoming new employees. And then it had been no more than a "Welcome to the Agency" and a formal handshake. She had been the most heavily recruited graduate in her master's class in computer science at Carnegie Mellon, with lucrative offers from Facebook, Google, Amazon, and half a dozen Silicon Valley luminaries. But a small notice on the job board in the university's Gates Center had caught her attention, promising a quieter, more intense and, in Amanda's mind, more significant spot in a cyber-world she knew she had access to only because of the government of the United States.

In 1968, Amanda's grandparents had sheltered US soldiers during the siege of the city of Hue in central Vietnam. It was an action that had eventually forced them from their home as the Northern People's Army swept south toward Saigon. A grateful American army secured passage for the couple and their ten-year-old son, Amanda's father, aboard a Navy rescue ship bound for Seattle. There, the family opened a flower shop, and later a restaurant specializing in Vietnamese cuisine to serve the burgeoning expatriate community escaping the failed war.

By 1980, three *House of Pho* eating establishments served Little Saigon in the city's International District, the largest of the restaurants managed by Amanda's second-generation parents. Through her teen years, the petite raven-haired waitress heard from one aged customer after another that she must someday repay the debt owed to her new country. The debt was compounded when a Gates scholarship supported the young prodigy through six years at

Carnegie Mellon, one of the nation's most prestigious computer science programs. The notice on the job board offered her what she viewed as the perfect opportunity to pay her country back.

Amanda had spent the year as a cyber operations officer, establishing a reputation as the CIA's rising star in the Directorate of Digital Innovation. The call from the director's personal assistant arranging a private meeting with the top man sent her precisely organized mind sifting back through the year, searching for some unrecognized blunder. She could think of none. The alternative, of course, was a new opportunity, a thought she found almost as unnerving.

Amanda realized early in life that she had a rare talent for instantly seeing patterns in what appeared to others to be chaos, while at the same time, developing elaborate codes that made ordered instructions appear completely random to those not privy to her designs. Perhaps the director wanted to take advantage of those skills. As she took the elevator to the top floor of CIA headquarters in Langley, Virginia, she struggled to bring order to what seemed an endless list of possibilities the meeting might present.

He greeted her personally at the door, showed her to a seat beside a glass-topped coffee table, and asked if she would like water, tea, or coffee. She declined. He sat opposite her without speaking for long enough to add to her apprehension, studying her thoughtfully as if he were still deciding what it was he had asked her there to discuss. When he finally spoke, there was at least a note of reassurance.

"You've quickly developed quite a reputation in cyber operations, Officer Nguyen. I've been impressed."

She nodded gratefully, sitting erect with hands in her lap as she had been taught to do in a household where every person her senior deserved her fullest respect.

He then moved the conversation in a direction that took her completely by surprise. "How sophisticated is your personal computer setup at home?" he asked.

Were they suspecting her of something? Did they think she was accessing internal systems from home? Sneaking out equipment or transferring classified information to her own hardware? She flushed self-consciously, a tiny prejudicial finger that had niggled at her since high school poking a tender spot in her brain. She pushed it aside, knowing she had nothing to hide. She answered honestly. "I have the best equipment I can afford."

"And what are you able to do with it?" The question scratched again at her tender spot.

"I'm not sure I understand. You must have something specific in mind."

The director smiled reassuringly. "Oh, you aren't suspected of anything, Officer Nguyen. But I need help with a special assignment and think you might be the right person to give me that assistance. But it can't be done from inside. It requires a top secret clearance, which you have, and absolute confidentiality between me and the officer working on it. No one else."

She gazed back at him silently for the same unnerving length of time. "I understand," she said finally. "But I am not sure what my home capabilities have to do with this."

He nodded an acknowledgment. "You will when I explain. Are you interested, and can I count on your complete discretion?"

"Is this legal?" she asked.

He chuckled lightly. "You know from your work downstairs that there are large gray areas in our work—and in what is legal. But as operations go, what I want to ask of you is completely legal."

"Then, yes. I am very interested."

He glanced absently out a window that provided the building's best corner view of the Potomac River, gathering his thoughts. When he spoke again, he told her what no other officer in the Central Intelligence Agency fully understood.

"About sixty years ago, at a time when all federal security

agencies were being widely challenged and receiving serious scrutiny by Congress, the public, and the media, the director at the time created a special branch—outside of both the organizational structure and management of the Agency. Only he and the president knew about it. According to lore handed down from one director to the next, for lack of a better name, it was called Unit One." He paused and studied Amanda who was trying her best to look thoughtful rather than display the *'This is incredible!'* thoughts that were racing through her mind.

"The Unit's task," he continued, "was to take care of assignments that were either too sensitive or too messy for us to handle internally—giving the CIA complete and credible deniability if something went awry. Are you following me?"

Amanda nodded. "Something like Mission Impossible," she murmured.

"Something like that," he said with a chuckle. "And they still exist. But over time, Unit One has become even more independent, if that seems possible. Some might even say 'rogue.' My only means of communicating with them is a highly encrypted phone call. No email. No text. Never a personal meeting. If I have an assignment, I call their team leader, a man who was initially called Fisher but now goes by the name Gabriel, and outline the assignment. They either let me know what information they need and I send it, or they come into our systems and get it themselves."

For the first time, Amanda showed visible surprise. "They have access to our internal systems?"

The Director nodded. "As much as we claim our internal networks are completely isolated, they are not. When they were set up, some access point was created. Don't ask me how or where. That's your area of expertise. But this portal gives Unit One and its own cyber geniuses access to everything we have. As our systems have been upgraded, that link has remained intact. As we're sitting here, they can come in and look at everything in our records and monitor every internal communication."

"*Why?*" Amanda gasped. "What was the idea behind that?"

"I think to begin with, there was some thought that they may need to serve as an internal inspector general, watching for corruption inside the organization. There was concern, I think, that our own IG position could be politicized and used at the discretion of either my office or the president's. And we've seen it happen. But I think primarily it was to allow this team to watch for issues we weren't willing to touch, and get something done about them."

"What wouldn't the CIA be willing to touch?" Amanda asked skeptically.

The Director shrugged. "Removal of a foreign head of state who was supposedly a staunch ally? Getting rid of a corrupt senior political figure in our own government. There are more of those situations than you would like to imagine."

"And they have done some of those things?"

He nodded and she arched her brow, inviting an example.

"Rescuing the Panchen Lama. Uncovering the manipulation that surrounded the Mehrens-Graves presidential candidacies. They've done some very useful work."

"So, what's the issue?" Amanda prodded, suspecting the answer, but not wanting to suggest it.

The director's face tightened into an irritated frown. "There have been other times when they've been a little *too* independent— and in a couple of cases, seemed to be working against us. One happened a few years ago at the time of the big Marburg epidemic in the Congo. Before you were with the Agency. Another might be happening now."

Amanda's forehead lifted a bit higher as the director's opening questions about her home equipment setup fell into place. "And you want to learn who they are and what they are up to, but need to do it from outside, where they can't monitor the search."

"Exactly," he said.

Amanda nodded, staring through the glass tabletop. "How many of them are there?"

"I don't know. There have been times when there were clearly three active in the field at the same time and one or two people feeding them information and coordinating what they did. So four or five, minimum."

"And you referred to these cyber-geniuses . . ."

The director again chuckled. "Yes. Whoever they are, the person or persons keep the link upgraded and hidden, work through our systems like they created them, and don't leave tracks. It's someone like you. Or like several of you. Their equipment has to be top of the line."

"How do they afford to operate?"

"You're aware, I'm sure, that we have what we call the 'black ops' budget, the portion of our appropriation each year that supports clandestine operations and doesn't show up anywhere. Well, let's say there are different shades of black. The darkest piece goes to Unit One—into an account where it is again transferred. I lose control over it at that point and can't track it. Who knows how much they spend and what they have stockpiled away."

Amanda smiled, mainly to herself. "If you're asking, Sir, what I think you are asking, I would be very happy to assist in any way I can."

"I'm asking three or four things," he admitted. "I'll be instructing your director to free you up to work directly with me. You'll be splitting your days—half down in your office and half at home. While here, I want you scouring our systems to find that backdoor or access point, whatever you people would call it, and watching for their activity in the system."

Amanda nodded.

"From home, where you will have permission to spend as much time as you need, I want you to begin unraveling the curtain that has shielded Unit One. I want to know who Gabriel is, who these computer gurus are, and who their field ops people are. This can't be outside of my control any longer. And I want to know where their base of operations is."

"Is there anything you can give me that would suggest a starting point?"

He stood and retrieved a thin manila envelope from his desk, handed it to her, but remained standing. She took it as a cue to stand with him.

"Here's what I know. Read it, make whatever secure notes you need, and return it to me. This all came to a head because we had an officer jump ship on us a decade ago in Syria, taking with him information that could seriously damage the Agency's reputation. He just surfaced again in Africa, and we're on his tail. But someone has been ahead of us at every step."

"And you think it's the Unit One people," Amanda ventured.

"That's what I think. But if it is, I don't know why. My theory is that this officer, a man named Nicholas Page, and someone in Unit One have some history. That will be a good place to begin your search. I've already ordered all communication about our hunt for Page to be by handwritten, personally delivered memo. I don't want them knowing *anything* about what we're doing in here related to this Page thing. I start my official day each morning at eight o'clock. I'd like to see you here in the office at seven. Will that work?"

She cringed internally, but nodded. That meant a five o'clock rollout.

"And no communication on this other than face-to-face in this office. Are we clear on that?"

"Yes, Sir. Very clear."

He extended his hand. "Then let's see what we can do to pull the covers off of Unit One."

25

They stood on a bare patch of clay between faded tire tracks until Yander and Taylor disappeared into the bush around a jog in the faint road. Adam watched Nick's face for a flicker of regret, but saw none.

"She not only agreed, she insisted," Adam said, swinging his pack and rifle across his back and feeling in a pocket of his cargo pants for his phone.

Nick scowled. "I knew she would balk as soon as we told her we were going to stay off the roads and keep moving west. A little discomfort, a little bad food, and a lot of walking was all she needed to convince herself she can make it to the coast without getting picked up—just because she's out of Zambia." He hoisted his own pack and weapon onto his shoulders and led them down through the scattered brush. "But I noticed," he added, grinning slyly back at Adam, "that you chose not to tell her you knew there are others looking for her."

"Or where we're really headed," Adam added. "They'll pick her up, question her about where she left us and where we're going, and keep watching Benguela. If she can remember the name of your cargo ship, they'll confirm your booking and expect us to try to meet it. All good for us. But I admit, I wasn't certain you'd be that willing to sacrifice her."

Nick snorted. "Hell, the other girls at the dig tried to warn me. And I had some second thoughts about helping take the damn bones out of the country. But she said she'd send them all back when she got the DNA samples she wanted. And I don't really care who has them in their museums. Do they belong to Zambia any more than anywhere else? Her claim is that we all have a little of that DNA in us, so I guess we all have some claim to them." He grinned back over his shoulder at Adam. "And after two days in the bush with her, I knew this wasn't a match made in heaven. Your little revelation last night that she has someone waiting for her up in Luanda really didn't surprise me. Her commitment to me was about as real as her hair color. It got pretty dark around the roots on about day three." He dodged a thick clump of coarse, waist-high grass. "Do you think she'll be able to convince Yander to get her on a bus to Luanda instead of Benguela?"

Adam chuckled. "When I gave him the money, I told him to send her wherever she wanted to go. He doesn't care. He might just turn her over to the police in Kuito, but I don't think so. The guy who found him for me gave me the impression they had both been UNITA fighters. I don't think he has much trust in government authority."

Adam had been poking at the satellite phone as he spoke, keeping an eye on Nick's steps and counting on his lead to avoid anything that shouldn't be stepped on. He raised the earpiece to his cheek and listened as they snaked through the bush, delaying breaking into a trot until after he made contact with Dreu.

"Hey, Cyclops," she said when she answered. "I hope you're not on your way to Luanda."

"We're not. Why?"

"Since the Agency started hiding their communication about Nick Page, I've had to work around them to figure out where their people are. I've been monitoring flight reservations from the airports in the country. Justin Turnley flew this morning from Huambo to the capital. Pollard took a flight up there last night. I'm guessing they discovered Taylor's friend is there, and they're going to just sit and wait for you."

"Taylor's on her way," Adam confessed. "We had a parting of the ways this morning."

"Permanently?"

"I hope so. We're south of a town called Cuemba, headed cross-

125

country to intercept the road south out of Kuito. I suspect it will take us about three days to get there. Is Manny out of Afghanistan?"

"Yes. We sent his list to Langley two days ago. You'd think the director would be grateful enough to show a little trust in us."

Adam chuckled. "He trusts us no farther than the next assignment. And from what you're telling me, he thinks he has good reason not to right now."

"Which he does," she agreed. "Do you need Manny?"

"See if he can meet us when we hit the Kuito road. And we need new documents. Nick's carrying a Canadian passport under the name Mark Alexander. It's in the Angolan system. You should be able to call it up and copy his photo onto new documents. Make something up showing him to be Jordanian. Then pull out my British set and have Manny bring them with him. Our plan is to go south into Namibia, so get some Namibian visas on them and plug us into their database."

She sniffed cynically. "And have them to you in three days?"

"Ah, you can have them all done by tomorrow," he chided. "That's all electronic now and you're the best. We can wait an extra day for Manny if we need to, but I'd like to get out of Angola pretty quickly if they're waiting for Taylor. She thinks we're headed for the coast, but they'll clamp down hard on this part of the country as soon as she tells them where we split—which she will. We figure she and the man who was guiding me will get to Cuemba tonight. Another day to Kuito or Huambo. Then plane or bus to the capital. I see her getting there day-after-tomorrow and being picked up immediately. So if Manny can get here by then, better for us."

"I'm calling him now," she said. "And will have the documents by the time he gets here. Anything else?"

"Yes. I assume your link into Langley is still intact."

"It seems to be. I can get in and find the information we normally look for. They've just gone silent about this search."

"They're using written memos and couriers," he guessed. "And I'm betting that means they're looking for you as aggressively as they're looking for us. Watch what you do."

"Like a hawk," she said.

"Any luck finding someone else who might be interested in Page?"

She paused and he heard her shuffle papers. "Kind of a long shot on this, but you might ask him if the name Severu Messina means anything to him."

"And why should it?"

"Messina is the man who made the hit in Syria when Nick refused. The rebels had been tipped off and Messina was captured almost immediately. Apparently, they really worked him over before he was traded as part of a prisoner swap."

"And you think he might blame Nick?"

"Nick apparently told the rebels there was going to be an assassination attempt. In some internal memos, Messina blames Nick for his capture and torture."

"And where is Messina now?"

"I've no idea," Dreu admitted. "Like we did, the man dropped out of sight years ago."

26

While she began to scour the architecture of the CIA's elaborate internal communications network looking for an access portal, Amanda Nguyen decided she would also launch a search for the infiltrator. Unit 1 had been accessing the system since the Agency first began to use digital technology, so the person involved in the initial design was most likely gone. It was possible this early cyber-spook had trained an internal replacement. It was more likely, though, that a small, select group like the director had described would go out looking for the best they could find. That meant the new genius behind the Unit's uncanny ability to know what was going on inside one of the most tightly guarded information systems in the world had to be someone with quite a reputation before joining this band of mavericks. Amanda began her search by looking for any highly regarded cyber-sleuth who had suddenly disappeared.

Reaching back fifteen years, she created a list of the most respected names in computer systems development, cyber-security, and digital larceny and ran the list through a program that traced any mention of each entry from year-to-year. When a name disappeared for a year, her program automatically scanned death records and looked for indications that the person had changed career or quietly retired. Within two days, she had a short list of five people who had once been viewed as among the world's best computer minds, but had suddenly dropped completely off the radar. One name immediately grabbed her attention. Dreu Sason.

The name had been mythic during Amanda's college days. Six years before Amanda competed, Dreu Sason of Stanford had led her team to a clean sweep of the national intercollegiate computer analytics competition. The Stanford group had been untouchable, largely because of a captain who in the lore of competitive collegiate systems design was remembered as being as brilliant as she was beautiful. The Carnegie Mellon coach had spoken about her with a kind of adoration that rankled Amanda and her teammates, as if this woman had been some kind of cyber-goddess.

"Ah, Dreu Sason," he murmured in one of their practice sessions. "The judges would present the problem, she would just sit and think about it for two or three minutes while her team waited, then give directions that led to two or three brilliant solutions while the rest of us were still charting possible approaches to the problem. She was amazing. . ." and he drifted off into reveries of what Amanda guessed was the woman's appearance as much as her brilliance.

A search of Dreu Sason's post-Stanford history revealed that she had taken a position with a company called FedTegrity that created cybersecurity systems for a number of the country's largest corporations and for most of the major branches of government. Amanda's antenna began to vibrate. When she read that FedTegrity's CEO, Marshall Ding, had been arrested for espionage based on information provided by an informant inside the company, and that Sason had later created her own company in Chandler, Arizona, which continued to service federal agencies, bells in Amanda's suspicious brain clattered like a three-alarm fire. Then Sason disappeared. She sold her interest in the Arizona business to her employees, and there was no mention of her in the past four years. When Amanda related the information during her first 7:00 a.m. meeting with the director, she could tell he was feeling good about his choice.

"You were with the Agency when the president of the cybersecurity company FedTegrity was arrested for inserting backdoor codes into government security systems," she reminded him when they were seated beside the glass coffee table. "What can you tell me about it?"

"Your reputation is well-deserved," the director said, smiling thinly. "That discovery was one of the Unit's successes."

"That discovery?"

The director frowned into the tabletop and rubbed at a spot on his forehead. "There was a group of ten Chinese children who came into the country through an adoption program in the late 1960s. The case records refer to them as the Weavers because they were initially raised and trained in a Cambodian village of silk weavers. The director at the time learned from the Unit One people that these children, as they grew, had systematically been nurtured into key corporate and government roles where they could manipulate major parts of our computer-dependent infrastructure, primarily the power grid."

"And Marshall Ding, the head of FedTegrity, was one of these Weavers?"

"One of the key people."

"And he was outed by someone internal, if I understand what I've been able to dig up."

The director chuckled. "I clearly chose the right person for this little assignment. But, yes. One of his principal designers recognized what he was doing and blew the whistle."

"Do you remember her name?"

"Her? You know that it was a woman?"

"I'm guessing. But if I could get that case record—or if someone here inside would know?"

The director reached for the phone on the table. "As I remember, Hagebusch was lead on the case."

Amanda raised a cautioning hand. "Just written memos. Remember, Sir?"

He bobbed his head apologetically. "He's now Deputy for Science and Technology and just down the hall. I'll ask him to come by."

Within minutes, Hagebusch knocked once, then stepped into the office. They rose to meet him, and the director introduced

Amanda.

"She's helping me with a special project," he acknowledged. "She thinks some information about the Weavers case you oversaw might be helpful. Amanda?"

"There was a whistleblower inside FedTegrity who gave evidence against its CEO," she began. "Do you happen to remember who that was?"

"Ah, yes," he said with a smile that reminded her of the team coach's nostalgic reminiscing at Carnegie Mellon. "A young woman. Dreu Sason."

27

Nick again cut limbs for a boma while Adam gathered wood, built a fire, and crafted a spit for a guinea hen he had dropped with an impressive headshot after they had decided on a camp site for the night. By the time the ring of thorns was high enough to be a deterrent, the hen sizzled over a glowing bed of coals and Adam had heated an MRE bag of what was labeled Bacon Hash Brown Potatoes.

As the night deepened and a cloudless sky began to sparkle with the southern constellations, Nick cut a drumstick from the bird and hunched cross-legged beside the fire.

"Ah," he mused, waxing philosophical. "The simple pleasures of two guys hanging out in the African bush. I've thought sometimes during the last two weeks that I could be pretty content to just stay out here. Maybe find some little village that would take me in, build a hut, find a woman who could tolerate me, and spend my days hunting with the men."

"You would hate it," Adam said with a wry grin, severing the other drumstick. "No clean water. No toilet in the hut. No light after sundown. After a month, you'd be begging for a hot shower and a cold beer."

Nick waved at the dark, wild expanse around them. "All those things are overrated. We've done just fine out here. And I could bring most of those improvements to the village if I decided I needed them. But look around you. No traffic noise. No smog. No one yanking your chain or worrying about who you've been or what you've done. Just life at its most basic."

Adam stripped the last of the meat from the bird's leg with his teeth and tossed the bone into the fire. "Tell me about Severu

Messina," he said.

Nick straightened, shook his head in disgust, and glared at his friend through the flickering blaze. "Where the hell did that come from?" he growled. "Great way to piss all over my little dream."

"You said 'no one worrying about who you've been.' I think someone might be worrying right now—even with you out here in the middle of this little Eden you've imagined for yourself."

"Where did you get the name?" Nick repeated.

"I told you I had good sources. And when I first started looking for you in this direction, a guy flew with me from Lusaka to Zambezi who I think may have been seeing if I could lead him to you. So I had my partner check to see if there was anyone other than the Agency guys who might want to find Nick Page. She gave me the name."

Nick leaned intently forward to stare through the fire. "What did this guy look like—the man on the plane?"

"About your height. Slighter build. Dark, wavy hair. Permanent five o'clock shadow. A slight limp. Spoke with an Italian accent."

"*Shit!*" Nick spit the word into the embers. "The accent's fake, but that sounds like Messina. He's the main reason I move every three or four years. The man's relentless. And someone inside the Company must feed him information."

Adam leaned over the bird, cut away a thigh, and relaxed back onto an elbow. "Tell me about him," he said.

Nick gazed off across the thorn barrier, his lips curling into a troubled sneer. A half-moon crested the eastern horizon, turning the scattered trees around them a skeletal white against the dark indigo of the night.

"He was a covert in Syria when I was. He does speak Italian like a native and must truly have some Italian blood. His cover was as a Sicilian businessman. Dealing in olive oil and Mediterranean nuts of some kind. I didn't even know he was Company until some of my Syrian friends, who suspected I was, asked me about him. I didn't confirm with Langley, but watched him over time."

"And when you refused to make the hit on the rebel leader, they called him in," Adam guessed.

The look of disgust on Nick's face deepened. "I *told* them what a damn foolish thing that was to do. Especially to hit Homsi. He was one of the opposition's most reasonable guys and would have been key to working out a non-violent solution. Langley said his popularity was exactly why they had chosen him. They said the 'people in our camp' wanted Assad gone, and Homsi's death would piss off the most people. I got a message to him before I split telling him he was being targeted. But I had no idea they would pass the job along to Messina."

Adam tossed more bones into the fire. "But they did, the rebels captured him, and he blamed you," he prompted.

"They caught him within minutes. I suspect they'd had people watching him after they decided he was CIA. I've heard he was tortured pretty badly before they figured out he might have value in a prisoner swap. To the guy's credit, he never admitted he was with the Company."

"I've never really understood that part of it," Adam admitted. "He was released back to the Syrian government. It was Assad's people who turned some captured rebel leaders back over to the freedom fighters in exchange for Messina."

Nick sniffed loudly. "The whole thing was screwed up. Our government told Assad that if his people would make the trade, then return Messina to the US, we wouldn't get as tough on the sarin gas thing as we had said we would. These damn wars are like murder trials, Adam. Plea bargains, deals cut, no admission of guilt, and only the general public gets screwed."

"How close has he come to catching up with you?"

Nick smiled thinly. "Close. I went to Morocco—Marrakesh— when I left Syria. Big sprawling city. Arabic speaking. The kind of place you would think you could disappear. I happened to look out the window of my second floor flat one morning and there he was. Standing in the street looking up at my place. I left through the back and kept on going. That's why one of these little villages looks so good to me. It would be hard for him to show up without being noticed, and I think the people would watch out for me."

"Visions of becoming a *bwana* with your own little fiefdom?" Adam suggested with a chuckle, trying to lighten the mood.

Nick shook his head seriously. "Nothing like that. I'd just like to disappear into one of them. Like our boma here, I could finally feel safe inside. I'm getting so tired of hiding. And I don't see this ending—ever."

Adam pushed up from his bag and added a few more sticks to the fire. "Well, let's get you out of here and away from your trackers," he said. "Then maybe you can circle back, find that woman you're looking for, and build your own ring of thorns."

28

Dreu reached Manny Beg at his parents' home in Houston. "I see you're living with your mother again," she teased.

"Checking in with the family before heading back to India. There's a nurse at the hospital up in Dharmsala that took care of me after I got shot up helping Britt get that lama out of China. I promised I'd come back to get better acquainted—sometime when you aren't interrupting my life with a job that might end it. I was just getting ready to head back. Do you have something for me?"

Dreu smiled at the constant willingness of their people to give up important plans at a moment's notice and go wherever they were needed. "If you don't mind detouring through Angola," she said, "I need to get documents and transportation to a couple of people—as fast as we can get them there."

Manny laughed into the phone. "Angola? Right on the way. And this sounds like just the kind of mission I was talking about. Where do I pick them up?"

"The people? Or the documents?"

"The stuff you want me to take."

"At George Bush International in two hours, if you can make it. A courier will meet you near the self-check-in kiosks for United Airlines with the package and a visa for your own passport. Watch for a tall, dark-haired woman wearing jeans and a Phoenix Suns T-shirt."

"What do I need with me?"

"Clothes for a hot climate. I'd plan on a week. Your international driver's license. I have money, a satphone, and complete instructions in the packet."

"Can you give me a capsule version?"

"I've got you booked in first class to Luanda. You're flying through Brussels and will be in the air about twenty-four hours, total. From Luanda you're on a flight to a city called Huambo, where you are going to buy a car so you can take it out of country. You'll call me when you have the car, and I'll let you know where you pick up your contacts. There are two, and they will tell you where they need to go."

"Will I need a weapon?"

"I can't say, though there are some people trying to track them down. If you need something, my guess is there's a lively arms market in Angola. And the men you meet will have some."

"Gotcha," he said. "I'd better start pulling things together. I'm nearly an hour from the airport."

"Take care, Manny. Call if you need anything."

Dreu punched the disconnect and slipped the phone into the pocket of her jeans. She had spent the morning putting finishing touches on the documents Adam needed and getting them in the Namibian system, then caught the early afternoon flight to Houston, booking Manny's flights while in the air. It had been one of those days when she hated what she did: forcing painstakingly exacting work into a tight schedule; hacking into systems that had to be entered without leaving fingerprints; using her preferred airline status to bump a passenger off an overbooked flight to Bush International in Houston. She felt like she was carrying a mission on her shoulders with absolutely no help. Planner, scheduler, courier, all in one. This was not the life she had bargained for when she signed on to share the Scottsdale apartment and every waking hour with Adam Zak.

She picked at the salad she'd purchased as a carryout from Ruby's Diner in the intercontinental terminal and thought about how her diet changed when Adam was away. She didn't take the time to fix or go out for anything really exciting, but snacked on chips and diet sodas at her computer. She cheated on her standard five mile run in the morning if she wasn't feeling up to it, cutting it back to three. Lately, that had been most days. And here she was, waiting for a man whose plans she had just disrupted, but who didn't hesitate because he believed everything she asked of him was important. Was Nick Page worth all this?

Fifty-three minutes after her call, she saw Manny enter the United check-in area. She had never met the man in person, but immediately recognized him from his picture and file description. His short, muscular frame reflected his family's Balti lineage in the high mountain Hunza Valley of Northeast Pakistan. But with his olive complexion and straight dark hair, he was often mistaken in the US for Latino. He walked with the confidence of a man who had survived Navy SEAL training and two tours in Afghanistan before being recruited into the Unit. He glanced quickly around the terminal area, hesitating briefly when he saw Dreu. It was not from recognition, she suspected, but because men typically found it difficult to look at her without a second glance. Or maybe it was the Phoenix Suns T-shirt. His eyes moved on until he felt he had a good sense for those around him. Dreu waited until he paused in front of the overhead display of arrivals and departures, then sidled up beside him. Even in low heels, she was a head taller.

"Mr. Beg?" she asked in her best imitation of a Spanish accent..

He turned and again gave her an appreciative look. "Yes. I'm Manny."

"This is for you." She handed him the thick envelope, turned immediately, and without looking back walked toward the sky train that would take her to her domestic flight back to Phoenix.

Manny watched her walk away, surprised the Unit would use such an eye-catching woman as a courier. Easy to remember and describe in detail. Then he carried the packet and his single carry-on into the nearest men's room, found a vacant stall, and reviewed the contents of the envelope. Two passports: one for a Jordanian named Ahmad Saleh; one for an Englishman, Daniel Hubbard. No doubt, aliases. Hubbard also had an international driver's license and Visa and Hilton Honors cards. Manny studied the Jordanian more carefully, wondering if the man's heavy beard hid a face that might trigger an alert if cleanshaven. It was the hard face of a man who was accustomed to keeping himself hidden.

The second man, Hubbard, was one Manny decided women would consider handsome. A long, angular face with hazel eyes, one slightly more closed than the other, and a hint of a smile that lifted the left corner of his mouth more than the right. His dark hair was neatly trimmed. The passport showed him to be thirty-eight.

Manny tucked the cards into his wallet, then slipped the passports into a pocket in an edge of his case where the luggage x-ray would be looking down on them and miss the thin books. When he had been recruited into the Unit, the man they called Gabriel had indicated Manny would usually be working alone. His last mission had been a solo dash up through the Uzbek villages of northern Afghanistan. But as part of his first assignment, the one that had placed him in the Indian hospital, he had shuttled prostitutes back and forth across the Khunjerab Pass between China and Pakistan, helping an attractive redhead and her moon-face guide smuggle a monk out of Tibet. Now he was picking up a Jordanian and Englishman in Angola. Hardly solo work.

He pulled stacks of new bills from deeper in the envelope and counted them quickly. Three $1000 bundles of $100 bills, five of fifties, and ten $500 packets of twenties. The eighteen thin stacks filled a canvas and Velcro money belt that he strapped about his hips where the walk-through arch of the TSA pre-check scanner wouldn't detect them. He knew he might still be singled out for a "random" pat-down—a randomness that his Pakistani looks and the name Manny Beg seemed to stack against him. But the TSA boys rarely checked his lower hips carefully, focusing instead on legs, belt area, and sides. If they found the money, he would simply explain that transferring funds into Angola was risky at best, ATMs were rare and unreliable, and he found it safer to carry what cash he needed to do business. Most TSA agents had little international experience themselves, wanted to be helpful, and accepted a plausible story.

The remaining items in the envelope were a first-class ticket to Luanda and instructions for picking up a used Ford Expedition in Huambo. The one-way fare and single carry-on bag would raise questions and increase the likelihood of the 'random' pat-down. But he had been through the routine enough times to know he could take care of that concern with, "I work for Conoco and am moving to Angola for a year. They ship everything we need in advance. It's all there waiting for me." He carried a bogus Conoco Executive Suites photo ID with a shadow image of the corporate Houston headquarters as background that he could flash if needed. In Houston, everyone knew Conoco and had seen the executive IDs. He had only used it twice. It had done the job both times.

A brief note told him that the 2006 Expedition had been purchased from a used car dealer in Huambo for 3,800,000 kwanza, or 6400 USD. The Unit had paid $3400 with a credit card, with a promise from the merchant that he and the vehicle would be at the airport when Manny arrived. He was to give the dealer the remaining $3000 in cash: three of the bundles in his belt. The salesman would have the title, keys, and an insurance policy the Unit was arranging while Manny traveled and would fax to the merchant.

"Start the car and do what you can to see that it is in good shape," the note advised. *"We've checked this dealer through several sources and he seems legit. He assures us the car is in good running order, will be fueled up, and will have 40 liters of fuel in containers in the back. Do what you can to verify before paying the balance."*

Manny chuckled, shook his head at the organization's ingenious solution to what most would see as mind-blowing challenges, and glanced at his watch. Thirty minutes until boarding. If he was lucky, this would be one of the new jets with individual cubicles and seats that reclined into beds. Aside from the inconvenience of a transfer in Belgium, he would be more than happy to sleep his way to Africa.

29

As her flight began its descent into the Angolan capital, Taylor Dennis whispered a silent prayer and, with the same breath, cursed the men who had left her to make her way solo halfway across the desolate country. By the time Matt Hylton, or whoever the hell he was, abandoned her on that path in the bush with that irritating little African, she had begun to suspect he was doubting the depths of her affection. But what did he expect? A guy whose face looked like the dark side of the moon couldn't really expect a woman like her to fall head over heels for him. He got what he wanted from her—a good lay every couple of nights—and when she'd had enough and cut him off out in that godforsaken badlands, he quit on her pretty damn fast. She should have played along with him until they were at least where she could leave him on her terms and find better help getting to Luanda.

And that Yander! The nerve of that man! He hadn't slowed for two minutes during their march to that excuse for a town. And he had refused to carry her pack, even when he could see she was barely able to drag herself after him. When they finally reached the collection of bullet-riddled buildings, he had planted her in what he called a guesthouse, a smelly pile of unpainted blocks with a family of five living in one room who charged her ten dollars to sleep in the other. She hadn't closed her eyes for a second during the night, listening to rats scurry across the floor in the dark, only to dash into wide cracks in the walls when she flipped on the single bedside lamp. Only the cockroaches had stayed out in the open.

He had shown up the next morning in time to rescue her from a breakfast of some gross-looking gluteny stuff they called *funje*, walked her without speaking to another square block building, and stuffed her into a packed bus headed for Huambo. The woman beside her had taken up two-thirds of the seat and held a runny-nosed kid on her lap during the smelly, smothering six-hour ride. The kid sat the entire time, licking snot from his upper lip and staring at her like she was some kind of space creature. She'd ridden with her face as close to the window as she dared, afraid to lay her forehead against the glass because it was so caked with grimy fingerprints she knew she'd come down with Ebola. At least Huambo had a decent hotel like the one the team had stayed at in Kabwe. She had camped for half an hour under a warm shower, eaten a meal that didn't taste like chemically heated soup kitchen leftovers, and slept in a real bed. It had taken every ounce of her resolve to force herself from under the covers for her 10:00 a.m. flight to the capital.

Airport security had been minimal, but she had still faced running her bag with four ossified bones through the scanner. She considered telling the security screeners upfront that she was an anthropologist taking samples to the national museum in Luanda. But she noticed that if a passenger asked the man beside the arched walk-through scanner a question in English, the woman watching the screen on the luggage conveyor took over the conversation and willingly let bags continue through x-ray unexamined while she spoke for her less communicative partner.

"Did I read that this city was a major coffee center before the war?" she asked as her bag approached the tunnel.

"Ah, yes," the woman answered, looking up at Taylor. "But it has been very difficult to continue much of the farming because so much of the country has landmines that have not been removed. But we still produce some of the best coffee in the world. You can buy some in the gift shop in the waiting area if you like."

"I believe I will," Taylor had promised, stepping quickly through the arch and scooping her bag from the belt.

The plane was only half full. She had paid for an economy-plus seat and ended up with a window and no one beside her. Thank

God for small favors! She had managed to sleep during most of the flight, anxious to join Wes fully rested. His texts promised her another hot shower, this one with a personal attendant who was anxious to soap her down, rub her clean with his body, and keep her awake during most of the night. He assured her that a hotel nearby offered a buffet with all the western food that, for the past months, she had been tasting only in her dreams. She was finally about to return to civilization.

Though near the front, she remained seated until the other passengers disembarked, then retrieved her bag from the overhead, made her way up the jet bridge and into the domestic arrival area. As she passed through sliding glass doors out of the secure zone, she saw him leaning against a column wearing neatly pressed tan pants, a flowered batik silk shirt, and loafers with no socks. He lounged casually with arms folded and an inviting grin on his patrician face. She hurried forward, throwing the strap of her bag over a shoulder to free her arms to wrap around the body she had been craving.

Along the windowed face of the terminal, a tall black man in neatly pressed dark pants, white shirt, and plain blue tie watched the woman arrive, then slipped through an outer door and called his partner.

"As the manifest indicated," he said to Pollard, "our Miss Dennis has arrived by herself. No sign of Page or someone I could identify as being Solomon."

"Follow them to the hotel," Pollard instructed. "We'll pick them up there. I think Miss Dennis isn't going to have the night she's expecting."

30

The message sent Dreu reeling back in her chair with her heart in her throat. She had entered the Agency's system to conduct her daily search of internal communication on anything related to Nicholas Page, Taylor Dennis, the countries surrounding Zambia, or Pollard and Turnley. The last few days had turned up nothing, but she felt compelled to check. The "nothing" had been so complete, in fact, that she was certain someone inside had ordered a shutdown on all electronic communication related to Page. But today his name appeared immediately and with it a note that, once she recovered from the initial shock, prompted her to pick up the satellite phone, enter half the number that would connect her to Adam, then set it back on the desktop while she gave more thought to what she had just seen.

The one-paragraph message was titled "re: Nicholas Page" but showed no office of origin. The words that had jolted her back from her screen began *Hello, Dreu Sason*. The rest of the memo only accelerated her heartrate.

At least, I am guessing it is you. I can't come up with anyone else who has the kind of expertise needed to hack this system who isn't either dead or living where I can find them. And your disappearance immediately following resolution of a Unit 1 assignment is just too coincidental! If it isn't you, I would welcome a correction. But know this. I am going to figure out how you get in here and limit that access. I must also warn you that you and your team, whatever names they are going by, need to stay out of the Nicholas Page business. You would all be better off to just quietly disappear once again.

She did need to alert Adam. But he would have questions, and she should at least try to find answers before she called. The first would be, "Any idea who this is coming from?"

She sat back, right elbow on the arm of her chair and thumb propped beneath her chin, staring at the screen. Supposedly, only the director knew about Unit 1. He, and the president. The most recent director had made it clear that he wasn't thrilled with having a loose appendage that itched where he couldn't scratch. But would he send something like this? It struck her as too casual. Too challenging. Not something directly from the DCI.

Despite her general distaste for the man who she viewed as pompous, politically ambitious, and a public grandstander, he had always struck her as completely committed to his office and to national security. If he decided to try to find out who was running this deep-cover irritant, she guessed he wouldn't even know how to set up the encrypted message she had just received—or realize she would have the tools needed to automatically decipher it. If he had involved someone else, he would only confide in the very few needed to expose the Unit. In fact, he would only need one person. Someone like her.

One of the weaknesses of an organization that is constantly suspicious is that it monitors everything, including itself. The only communication that isn't recorded is conversation between people in unofficial settings and handwritten memos that are intentionally meant to be "off the record." That meant that every call made by the director, his administrative assistant, or support staff was logged and recorded. Dreu began there, looking for a scheduled meeting between the director and someone from Cyber Operations or Digital Innovation within the last week—most likely, one of the highly talented trench workers. It took only fifteen minutes to find the name she was looking for: Amanda Nguyen, a junior cyber-operations officer.

Dreu exited the system and initiated a Google search for Amanda Nguyen, immediately finding a dozen. One was a prominent civil rights activist and champion of victims of sexual assault. Another, an equity analyst for Bloomberg. A third was vice president of accounts for a Fortune 500 company. A talented group, these Amanda Nguyens! Dreu limited her search to those with academic backgrounds in computer systems analysis and immediately hit paydirt. Gates Scholar and *summa cum laude* graduate. Undergrad and master's degrees from Carnegie Mellon's prestigious Computer Sciences program. Post-graduation employment? Unknown.

It took all of her willpower to keep from firing back a "Good morning, Amanda," to let the woman know that two could play at this game. But she knew she first needed to visit with Adam. His second question would be, "How much do you think they know about us?" And the third, "Can she figure out how you are getting into their network?" She doubted Amanda knew other specific names, or she would have dangled one out as evidence they were getting close to uncovering the Unit's secrets. The third question? Amanda would be aware that an entry portal had been created in the system's architecture, but it would be virtually impossible to find without understanding exactly where to look and what to do once the location was found.

Dreu's predecessor Anita, a Cuban CIA informant who had fled the island following the failed Bay of Pigs invasion, had helped the Agency create a digital network during the pioneering decade of the 1960s. She had been the genius behind inserting the initial "backdoor" into the system that had linked Unit 1's fledgling operation, then located in a rural ranch-style home outside Ashburn, Virginia, to all internal CIA files. As the Agency's systems grew and transitioned from early FORTRAN to the latest, more security-conscious languages and architecture, Nita's fertile brain had stayed a step ahead, keeping an active access portal ingeniously hidden. It was now imbedded in the CIA's Office of

Public Affairs *Weekly Summary,* a publicly available announcement that made declassified Agency information available to the public.

Each declassified file had an elaborate thirty symbol number. By entering three of these codes, separated by commas, into the Freedom of Information Act query box, Dreu was now able to enter the Agency's encrypted internal files, including those that created and disseminated daily encryption and deciphering keys. At the end of each venture into the system, a random number generator of her own design selected three new codes for the next access. Her computer was programmed to use the string of numbers to open the portal, then again divide the three individual component codes to make it appear that separate queries had been made, intentionally spaced between other requests. To anyone scanning the network for intruders, the entries were no longer successive on the log, but appeared to arrive as separate entries from three of the hundreds of reporters and researchers who daily requested access to the files. Even with an understanding of how it was done, without the actual codes and specific order, it was virtually impossible to identify the three components that made up a day's combination.

She drew a deep breath to calm her racing heart, logged out of the machine that had given her the game-changing message, and called Adam. He was out of breath when he answered.

"Sorry," he panted. "We're within a mile or two of the road coming south out of Kuito. We're trying to get to it and set up camp before it gets dark. We've been moving at a steady jog."

"Can you listen while you run?" she asked.

"Yeah. I might need to stop to answer. What do you have for us?"

"Well, this is the proverbial 'good news, bad news.' First, the good news. Manny is on his way and should reach you early tomorrow morning, your time. He has the documents you asked for. When you get set up, call me with your exact coordinates so I can guide him to you and give you a better ETA."

"That's . . . very good . . . news." She could tell he hadn't slowed. "Have you . . . heard anything . . . about Taylor?"

"No. There's still an internal blackout on everything related to Nick or the search. And that's where the bad news comes in." She paused and the sound of his footfalls stopped.

"When I entered the Agency's system today and initiated a search for current info concerning Nicholas Page, a message immediately came up that said "Hello, Dreu Sason.""

"Oh, shit," Adam swore into the phone. There was a long pause while he steadied his breathing. "Any idea who it came from?" There it was. Question number one.

"Like we've suspected, the director must think we're interfering in this search and is hunting for us. I guessed he would need someone inside who was talented enough to try to figure out who we are, how we get into their system, and where we are located. He's only called one person from Digital Innovation to his office this week, and she fits the bill. An all-star grad from Carnegie Mellon named Amanda Nguyen."

Adam sniffed into the phone. "Hmm. Vietnamese surname. Her family name or a married name?"

"Family name. She's third generation. Her grandparents were from Hue and were pulled out of Vietnam after Tet."

"She'll be loyal, disciplined, and committed," Adam mused. "She has to be guessing at who you are, but did some clever work to figure that out. Do you think she has names for anyone else yet?" Question two—right on schedule.

"I think she would have thrown out a name or two if she had them," Dreu answered. "But if I were in her shoes, I'd be tracing Nick's history for a link to someone he knew who might have disappeared into the Unit. It won't take long for her to come up with Tom Mercomes. If the men who've been chasing you questioned the anthropologists very carefully, they will probably know that the Mr. Solomon who showed up at their dig site had a prosthetic eye. I'd give them no more than two days before they're looking for you by name."

"Wrong name, though," Adam reminded her. "And changed appearance. I'll try not to look anyone directly in the eyes if we need to clear customs or cross borders."

"Don't be flip about this," she warned irritably. "They're after us and know what Nick looks like. As long as you're in Africa, they have the advantage."

"With you and Manny, I'd take my chances any day," he said lightly. "Do you think this Amanda can figure out how we get into the system?" Question three, as anticipated.

Dreu shook her head into the phone. "No way. Unless she figures out it's through the FOI Act query box and they shut that down completely, I don't think they can close us out."

"Well, I'll call when we get set up tonight and tell you exactly where we are. What are you going to do about Amanda? I definitely wouldn't confirm your identity."

Dreu hadn't yet decided what she was going to do. "I won't," she agreed. "But I might try to see what I can get her to tell *me*."

31

Manny reached Huambo at 6:30 in the evening on the return flight of the 737 that had carried Taylor Dennis to the Angolan capital earlier in the day. In a restroom inside the arrival area, he slipped again into a stall, unloaded $3000 from his belt, and sealed the money in an envelope he had requested from the attendant during the flight from Brussels. He was one of the last through a cursory immigration and customs check. A heavy African in a wrinkled white shirt with splayed buttons and a belly that hung loosely over his belt waited as Manny exited the secure area, expectantly holding a hand-lettered sign that said "Mr. Beg". Manny introduced himself in English, extending a hand.

"Ah, yes. Mr. Beg!" the fat man said in accented English, with a handshake that quivered up into the man's fleshy shoulder. "I have the car waiting for you. Please come this way." He turned and, with what seemed Herculean effort, threw his considerable bulk into motion, waddled out of the terminal and across the drop-off access road. Near the back of the terminal parking area, a freshly washed white Expedition sat beside a Toyota 4-Runner of the same color. The man molded a super-sized hip against the fender of the Toyota, panting and waving a chubby hand at the Ford.

"Here it is," he said breathlessly. "Very good condition." He again forced himself into motion, unlocked the 4-Runner, and lifted a thick envelope from the passenger seat. "Keys and papers are here, with insurance your office sent to me. Our agreement is that you will pay three thousand American dollars now, and the car is yours."

Manny opened the envelope, drew out the electronic key, and punched the Expedition's unlock. He reached in and popped the hood. "I would like to check the oil and start the car before we settle this," he said. "Make sure all the systems work."

"Of course," the man agreed with a nod that sent ripples down through the sagging wattle of chin. He mopped his brow with a folded white handkerchief. "You will see that all is in good condition. The car has had only one owner—the wife of an Australian who has been here for many years."

These guys are the same everywhere, Manny thought and lifted the hood. The oil was clean and full, the engine ran smoothly, and the 98,000 miles showed relatively light driving for the car's age. He climbed from behind the wheel, fished the envelope of money from his pocket, and handed it to the merchant.

"Three thousand in cash. Please give it a quick count. Everything appears to be just as you said it would be."

The man's plump fingers showed remarkable dexterity as he thumbed through the bills. He nodded, again gave Manny's hand a vigorous shake, and opened the driver's door of the Toyota. "Thank you for your business," he said, hoisting his mass onto the fully extended seat and pulling the door after him. He backed the 4-Runner out of its spot, gave a friendly wave, and cut diagonally across the parking area toward the exit.

Manny slid into the Ford, activated his satphone, and punched in the Unit's number, turning on the speaker function. The woman who had called him about the assignment answered immediately.

"I'm here and have the car," he said simply. "Everything looks to be in good shape. Do you have coordinates?"

"I do." As she read a series of numbers, he entered them into a GPS app on the phone.

"I'm probably two and a half hours away from there," he reported, studying the readout. "Have them watching for me around ten—unless I see some reason to deviate. If there's a change, I'll call you."

"Understood," she said. "My impression is that this is out in the middle of open bush country."

"It looks that way to me."

"I just didn't want you to get there and expect to see a building or anything. If you don't see them immediately, pull off, flash your lights, and stand in front of the car where they can see you."

"Roger," Manny replied. "On my way."

32

Pollard and Turnley approached the pair of hormone-charged anthropologists as soon as they entered the foyer of the International Hotel, cutting short any hope of a soapy shower and pre-lunch romp in the sack. The officers flashed their CIA credentials, suggested the couple not make a scene in the public lobby, and ushered them down a side hallway to a pre-arranged meeting room. Wesley Epling immediately argued that the men had no jurisdiction in Angola, a claim to which Pollard readily agreed.

"You are absolutely right," the agent conceded. "But I can assure you that you will find it much more pleasant to cooperate with us than with the Angolan national police. And our interest isn't in you or Taylor, but in the man she left Kabwe with. In fact, we really don't give a damn about whatever it is Taylor took from the site, as long as she helps us find the man she knew as Matthew Hylton."

When Epling insisted he would like to see that in writing before Taylor chose to cooperate, Pollard answered with, "Listen, professor. The both of you are in one shitload of trouble. You can help us out and make it a lot easier on yourselves, or act like assholes and make us do the same. I might remind you that your fiancée here is a wanted person in Africa and that we're in Angola. Not Providence, Rhode Island. We walk out of here and you're on your own, aiding and abetting a fugitive." He then invited Turnley to escort the suddenly more cooperative academic to his room and keep him company while Pollard talked to the woman.

"As I said," he told Taylor when just the two faced each other across the table, "you were pretty stupid to take off with something from the dig, but I don't give a damn about your bones. As far as I'm concerned, you and your friend can see if you can get them out of the country, just as you were planning to. Unless, of course, you decide you don't want to help us. Then you can both find out what it's like to spend a few nights in an Angolan prison while Zambia tries to extradite you. And I think they might invite you to spend ten to twenty years with them. I can assure you, that won't be something you want to experience. Now, can we talk?" He placed a small digital recorder between them.

"What do you want with Matt?" she asked.

"That's nothing you need to trouble yourself with. And you're better off not knowing. Let's just say we've been looking for him for a long time."

"I don't know where he is. He dumped me out in the bush with some sadistic little African man."

"Sadistic? Did he harm you?"

Taylor rolled her eyes. "You should see my feet. Blisters the size of fried eggs. And the man hardly even stopped to let me pee for a whole day. I need to get bandages on these sores or they're going to get all infected."

"Then let's get on with where it was he left you with this thoughtless little African," Pollard suggested. "Was anyone else with you?"

"The African and some tall white man found us a couple of days ago. Someone Matt knew. But Matt seemed really surprised to see him. I don't think he knew they were coming."

"Did this man have a name?"

"Matt called him Cyclops."

"Cyclops? No other name?"

"No. Not that I remember. But he called Matt 'Nick.'"

Pollard nodded and glanced at the recorder. "You didn't hear the name Solomon mentioned?"

"No. The African's name was Yander. I do remember that."

"And they just found you out in the bush? Did they say *how* they found you or where they'd come from?"

Taylor shook her blonde head. "No. We were trapped by these hyenas, and they just appeared all of a sudden—and shot two of them. After that, they didn't talk much when I was around."

"I would think you would have been around all the time."

She scowled across the table. "I mean *right* around. When we were walking, they would stay far enough ahead or behind that we couldn't hear."

"You mean, you and Yander."

"Yeah. Yander didn't talk much either. And when we camped, Nick and Cyclops would go off and talk."

Pollard nodded. "Tell me about when you split up."

She slumped back in her chair, dropped her hands into her lap, and gazed grimly at a stylized painting of three African women with baskets on their heads that adorned one of the walls. "We came to this trail late in the afternoon two days ago. What Yander called a road. But it was really no more than tire tracks through the bush. He said it was the road to some town and that we could be there the next day."

"Do you remember the name of the town?"

She thought for a moment, mouth pursed. "No. I stayed there overnight. It was a *horrible* place. Rats and cockroaches and this food that was like paste." She gritted her teeth and a long shiver shook her thin shoulders. "I don't remember what he called it. I think it started with a C or a K."

"Kuito?"

"No. I went through Kuito on the bus on the way to the airport. It was on the other side of there."

"And it took you most of a day to walk to this town with Yander after you split. Is that right?"

"Yes. We got there maybe about four or five in the afternoon."

"Why did you split up?"

"Oh, where should I start?" she said with a disgusted snicker, looking off again at the painting. "For one thing, we'd been hiking through that godforsaken bush for a week, sleeping on the ground, chased by a pack of hyenas, and eating the most godawful stuff that Matt had in these pouches. When Yander said we were within a day of a town, I said we needed to go there, even if we got caught. I'd had enough."

"But Matt and this friend weren't willing to do that?"

She gave her head a slow, dramatic shake. "Oh, no. They were going to stay off the roads all the way to the coast."

"Is that where they said they were going? To the coast?"

"Matt said he'd arranged for us to catch a cargo ship at some port there. A captain who would take us onboard without worrying about who we were or why we wanted out of the country. The last I saw of them, they were headed off in that direction."

"To Benguela?"

"No. That wasn't it. Something shorter."

"Lobito?"

"Yes. That was it. Lobito."

"Do you remember the name of the ship?"

"No. He never told me. I think he didn't trust me with some of that information—in case we got caught."

"Like now," Pollard couldn't resist saying.

"Yeah. Like now."

"I would imagine the port would check passports, even if you were leaving on a cargo ship. You weren't worried that your names would be recognized?"

Taylor stretched back on her chair and fished into a front pocket. "Matt got these for us," she said, sliding the Canadian document over to Pollard. "He flew down to Johannesburg not too long after we started planning this and got them from some guy he knew there. He said they were for real people and would get us through. And I think he didn't expect them to be checked very carefully. I mean, this was a cargo ship, not some cruise liner."

Pollard picked up the passport and flipped to the photo page. "Linda Griffith. Vancouver. Do you remember what name he was using?"

"No. I didn't see his. We were going to go over all this again before we got to the ship."

Pollard arched a skeptical brow. "But your friend was meeting you here."

Taylor again leaned forward, elbows on the table, a disgusted smirk twisting her surly lips. "Well, you see, we weren't supposed to crash. And as soon as he got me to the coast, I was going to get us checked into a hotel, give Matt something to help him sleep, and catch a flight up to Luanda. Wes and I had it all worked out. And then that imbecile landed us in the middle of nowhere. Change of plan."

"He's supposed to be a very experienced pilot. And you were probably lucky to even be able to walk away from the plane," Pollard commented.

"Well, he landed it on the riverbank and we covered it all up."

"Yes. We found it. That's what led us to you."

She raised a surprised brow. "Oh, really? How did you find it?"

"That's also something you don't need to know. Now, let's figure out where you split up." He pulled a map from the thin case that had held the recorder and spread it in front of her. "You say you came through Kuito on the bus." He pointed to the first town to the east. "Camacupa?"

"No. That doesn't sound right."

"Cuemba?"

"Yes. That's it. Cuemba."

"And you would have hiked up from the south, I assume. You walked pretty steadily for about a day?"

"*Very* steadily."

"From sunup?"

"Right at sunup."

"So that would be about nine hours. Let's figure twenty to twenty-five miles."

"At least," she said. "And we had been following a river before we split."

Pollard looked down again at the map, gave a quick nod, and folded it carefully. "I think that's all for now. I'm going to send you up to your room, and I want you and your friend to stay here until we're through with you. You leave and we won't protect you anymore. In fact, we will have the local authorities all over you. Are we clear on that?"

She nodded grimly.

"Alright. Head on up and ask Officer Turnley to join me. And stay put, or there's no deal."

With Turnley back in the room, Pollard again spread the map across the table.

"She said they split somewhere south of Cuemba along a river," he told his partner, pointing at the city on the chart. "Probably twenty or twenty-five miles. Nick and our mystery man continued west cross-country. She claims they were going to stay off the roads until they reached the coast."

Turnley shook his head skeptically. "Maybe as far as the road to Kuito," he guessed. "But if they know Angola at all—and I think Page probably did his homework—I doubt he planned to go farther than that."

Pollard looked up with a curious frown. "Why not? I'd think they would want to stay out of sight as long as they can. They seem pretty capable of surviving in the bush."

"Mines," Turnley said simply. "Huambo was the center of UNITA activity during the civil war. The whole country west of Kuito still has landmines all over it. This is one of the most heavily mined places in the world, and most are still in the ground. I've read estimates of ten to twenty million, mainly in the western half. Once they cross that road, they're headed right into the area of greatest concentration."

Pollard leaned over the map. "And you think they'll know that?"

"If he studied the route he was planning at all, that would be a pretty major oversight."

"But he was planning to fly *over* all this." Pollard swept a finger across the chart from Zambia to the coast.

"Do you think so?" Turnley asked with a cynical grin. "An expert pilot. No engine trouble while still over Zambia, then failure a hundred miles into Angola when he had a nice flat riverbed below? A woman who was planning to ditch him, and a friend who shows up within days of the time they're on the ground?"

"But when Solomon talked to the people at the dig site, he didn't seem to know where Page had gone," Pollard objected.

"At least, that's the impression he gave," Turnley pointed out. "And they told him Page had gone east. But he immediately went west—and took that chopper pilot right to the crash site."

Pollard straightened over the map. "Then why even go to the dig? Why not head directly to the plane?"

Turnley mulled the question over for a moment. "Maybe he wanted to know what the woman had with her," he offered.

Pollard shook off the suggestion. "He could learn that when he found them. And he had to know he was risking exposure by going to Kabwe. I don't believe he knew where they were. Taylor just told me Page seemed genuinely surprised when Solomon showed up—assuming it was Solomon."

"Yes. Assuming," Turnley agreed. "So how do we find the sons-a-bitches?"

"If you're right about the mines, they either turn toward Kuito when they hit this road," Pollard said, stabbing the map with a finger, "or we may not need to worry about them."

"Or they go south," Turnley suggested. "To Namibia. What's our move?"

"Contact the national police. Ask that they put out an APB for two western men, one on a Canadian passport fitting Page's description and one an American named Robert Solomon. Alert the station at the border with Namibia. Then I suggest we go to the port of Lobito and find out what ship he booked two berths on. My guess is that they will come up to Kuito, then work their way to the coast and try to reach that ship."

33

Dreu Sason sat back, arms folded, and stared thoughtfully at her screen. She was in the system, as far as she knew, undetected. But if she were Amanda Nguyen—and the more she reviewed internal activity involving the director's office, the more certain she was that her new nemesis was Amanda—she would have a program watching for any activity initiated by a computer that wasn't part of the authorized network. As soon as Dreu entered, Amanda would be alerted. So—how should she play this? Commandeer and work through an authorized IP address that would disguise her entry? That would only delay discovery until Amanda saw her looking for information related to the Africa search. Take on the cyber-operations wonderkid directly? Dreu had never been one to shy away from a challenge. In fact, this little head-to-head with Cyber Officer Nguyen had suddenly made the whole Nick Page thing more than sheer drudgery. She leaned forward, poised her fingers over the keys, and said aloud, "Okay, Miss Nguyen. Let's see what you're made of."

Hello, Amanda, she typed. *I'm not sure who you think is on this end, but I'm pleased to see some real talent on that end.*
She sat back and waited. Seven minutes later the reply came.

Hello, Dreu. And I am fairly certain it is you. FedTegrity? The Weavers case? You disappear afterward with all that federal cyber-security knowledge. Tell me I'm wrong.

Lots of inferences there, Dreu answered. *Let's just say this is 'Fisher.'*

The reply was immediate. *Fisher's dead. As you know, Gabriel now runs the Unit.*

Dreu frowned into the screen. *Unless you are the director, someone has been talking out of school.*

And some black ops unit has been misbehaving out of school. The Director is not pleased.

There is no school, Dreu entered. *Our mission is to do what is best for the country when your people don't seem to be able to get the job done.*

Oh, testy! And how is hiding Nick Page in the best interest of the country?

Nick Page?

Please, Dreu. Let's get past all the dancing around and save ourselves some time. We know you have someone—a Mr. Solomon—working to keep Page out of our hands. That's not exactly team play.

Dreu again eased away from the machine. Was there anything to be gained by playing coy? Probably not. *Then explain to me how bringing Page in, or getting rid of him, is in the nation's best interest. He's a threat to you because he can embarrass the great, sacred Company. Disclose some bad missteps. Am I wrong?*

There was a long enough pause that Dreu had to wonder if Amanda really knew why the Agency was pursuing Nick. Then, *The reasons are not my concern. Your disregard for Agency programs, policy, and protocols is.*

Your policies and protocols have never been ours, Dreu keyed in. *We were created to be arms-length. Independent in action and judgment.*

But to exercise good judgment—using our resources, Amanda replied.

Dreu nodded to herself. *We believe we are. That is always our guiding beacon.*

Another lengthy pause, then, *Who is Tom Mercomes?*

The question hit her with the same gut punch as the initial "Hello, Dreu Sason." She gulped a breath, leaning back and pursing her lips. It was time to end the candor. *Not a name I recognize.*

Really? Air Force friend of Nick Page who Nick saved after an accident? Mercomes lost an eye. Might account for the nickname 'Cyclops.'

Dreu shook her head. This woman had been digging deep—and fast! *You've lost me, Amanda. Give me a little help here.*

How about a little help from you first—like how you get in here.

We have always had access. And it has been authorized as part of our mission.

Then why hide it so deep? We could simply grant you standard privileges to all information.

And be able to cut us off when you get bent out of shape about something. I believe that's why the initial arrangement was for carefully disguised access that only we know about.

That's the problem here, 'Fisher.' No trust!

And it's trust that has shut down all internal communication concerning the Page hunt? Give me a break! And what do you really know about who Page is? And why they are after him?

Another pause.

Let's just leave it at this for now, Amanda entered after a moment. *We're closing in on Page. If you have someone with him when we find him, your man will also be treated as a threat to the Agency.*

Drew took her own time replying. As she did, she wondered how upset Adam would be with her response. *And we'll leave it at this,* she typed. *Nick Page is not the only person aware of the Syria debacle. What he knows, others know. And they have the best interests of the nation at heart. We would all be much better served if you left him alone.*

So now we're down to threats, came back the reply. *Remember who you are dealing with.*

Dreu again shook her head at the screen. *Oh, Amanda,* she wrote. *You are so new to all of this!*

34

Thirty-one kilometers south of the city of Kuito, Manny Beg eased the Expedition onto the unpaved shoulder and braked to a stop, leaving the engine running. He double-checked the coordinates against those the caller had given him, saw no headlights in either direction, and flashed his own off and on three times. Leaving the beams on low, he climbed casually from the Ford, stretched beside the open driver's window, then walked into the cones of light and made a slow turn. The night was eerily dark and silent. When he gazed beyond the beam, no lights glowed in any direction but up. Overhead, the sky glittered with such an array of stars that he had the disorienting feeling that he was gazing *up* at an endless city of lights. The sound of footfalls on the pavement behind him pulled his thoughts back to the deserted road. A flashlight stabbed at him from the darkness.

"Manny?" a man's voice asked.

"At your service," he replied. The flashlight went out and two men, both a head taller, moved forward into the headlights. He recognized the heavily bearded Jordanian from his passport picture as Ahmed Saleh. The second man, the one who held the light, had a broad-brimmed hat pulled low over his face that revealed only a lop-sided grin.

"Thanks for coming for us," he said, extending a hand. "Let's get moving. We've got about nine and a half hours to the border and plenty of time to get acquainted. Do you have extra gas?"

Manny nodded toward the rear of the SUV. "Forty liters. It's stinking up the car. We'll still need to stop in Menongue to fill everything up. If we keep driving, we should be able to reach Namibia by ten o'clock."

"We have some shopping to do in Ondjiva," the hatted man said, leading them around the vehicle to throw packs and weapons into the back. "And we may need to get a room for a couple of hours. We need to wash up and get into clean clothes before we cross the border."

The bearded man climbed into the rear seat. The Englishman, identified by his passport as Hubbard, took the passenger seat beside Manny who had to agree that a bath was in order. He eased the Ford into drive and steered back onto the pavement, heading south.

"Where are we headed?" he asked, checking his mirrors for other traffic and seeing none.

"Windhoek," the bearded shadow in the rear seat replied. "I have a contact in Johannesburg who flies cargo all over this part of Africa and up into Europe. For the right money, I believe I can get him to make a run into Windhoek to pick us up, then ferry us into Europe somewhere. We just needed to be able to tell him when and where to meet us, and where we want to end up."

"How far beyond the border is Windhoek?" Manny asked.

"Another eight hours with no stops."

"So maybe late tonight if we keep driving," Manny estimated.

"That's the plan," the man beside him said with no trace of an English accent. "But this could all change. I don't know how much you were told by Gabriel, but we need to get safely out of Africa. And we know there are some pretty capable people trying to stop us. Right now, we believe they think we're headed for the Angolan coast. But they have good sources of information, and we can't count on them not figuring out we went south."

"I spoke to a woman," Manny said. "My instructions were to pick up the car, find you two, and follow your instructions."

"Then you're pretty much up to speed," the man calling himself Hubbard said. "But it's about time to check in and get an update." He pulled a phone identical to Manny's from his pocket and punched numbers on its face.

167

The call was immediately more casual than any conversation Manny had ever had with the Unit.

"We've been picked up," Hubbard said when the call was answered. "Nick's got a contact in South Africa who flies commercial cargo. A man named Ajani Botha. Nick believes the guy will pick us up in Windhoek for the right price and take us into Europe."

Hubbard listened, then said, "He thinks two hundred thousand will do the job. A hundred in advance and a hundred when we're safely delivered. Nick will call to make the arrangement, and I'll let you know where to wire the money if this works out." The three men in the Expedition sat silently while Hubbard listened, his face darkening in the dim glow of the dash lights.

"Damn," he muttered under his breath, then more clearly into the phone, "This woman must be good. And the endgame sounds like it's to expose us all, not just get to Nick. Have you sent anything back?" Again he listened.

"Hmm," he grunted. "Hard to know if that will quiet them or convince them they need to work harder to get rid of us. What's the status on Britt and Tony's projects?" Hubbard turned to gaze into the blackness of the passing bush, nodding as he was given the update. After the indistinct murmurings of what Manny judged to be a woman's voice ended, Hubbard sat quietly for a long moment, still staring into the night.

"Tell them to finish up what they can and get back into the country," he said finally. "If this all comes unraveled, we need them close to home. I'll call again when we've crossed the border. By then, I should have information about the flight out. It may be early morning for you." He listened for another moment, then said more quietly, "Yes. Same here. Talk to you later."

Manny kept his eyes on the strip of gray asphalt illuminated by his headlights, processing the realization that the man who sat beside him was the one who gave the orders at Unit 1. His passenger was Gabriel. And for some reason that seemed to be upsetting people elsewhere, the top guy had decided to come find the man in the center seat—who was apparently named Nick. Was he another Unit agent? If one of them got in trouble, did the head man come out after them? Manny knew it had to be more than that. One of his first assignments had been to go to the rescue of Britt Haugen in Western China, the same Britt he guessed had just been mentioned in the phone call. And it sounded like Gabriel was ordering everyone back into the country. As he began to mull over possible reasons, Hubbard spoke to Nick, giving him part of the answer.

"Someone inside the Agency's asking about Tom Mercomes," he said, turning his head enough that Manny knew the comment was directed to the man behind him.

"No shit," the bearded man muttered. "I thought you told me Mercomes had no history. All purged."

Hubbard turned more directly to Manny. "To keep this from getting totally confusing, we need to catch you up on a few things," he said. "My name's Adam. Adam Zak. This is Nick Page in the back. We worked together years ago, and Nick's gotten himself into a bit of trouble with some influential people in Washington. Let's just say he knows some dirty secrets they don't want exposed. I'm with Unit One and was sent to find him and get him somewhere safe. As it turned out, the Washington people figured out where he was about the same time I did, and we needed help. You're the help."

Manny nodded, then grinned over at Adam. "From your phone conversation, it sounded like you're more than just one of us."

"Hmm. Yeah," Adam muttered. "For now, let's leave it at 'I've been where you are and have a different assignment now.' But we all have the same objective. Nick needs to disappear again, and we all need to get safely out of Africa. And someone inside the CIA is working hard to keep that from happening."

"And this Mercomes is one of the two of you before you disappeared the first time," Manny guessed.

"Right," Adam confirmed without indicating which. "An identity we thought had been completely erased. And the fact someone is trying to uncover it raises some greater concern about what else they're trying to find out, and why."

"All I really need to know," Manny agreed. "Thanks for bringing me up to speed—and for bringing me in on the rescue."

Adam turned his attention back to Nick. "Our person told whoever's poking around into our pasts that a number of people know the story behind your leaving Syria. Silencing you won't silence the story, but will force it out."

"And what was the reply?"

"The person said, 'Remember who you are dealing with.'"

"Just what I'd expect," Nick muttered. "As if we could somehow forget."

In Ondjiva, forty kilometers from the Namibian border, they used Manny's credit card to pay $35 for a room at the only hotel they could find, a place called the Águia Verde, then found a shop that sold canvas pants, long-sleeved khaki shirts, and acceptable socks and underwear. They showered and Manny and Adam shaved while Nick trimmed and squared his beard to hide and reshape his face. Ninety minutes later, they stepped into line behind a group of a dozen European tourists bound for Etosha National Park. Adam listened to the conversation ahead of him, then took the lead as the three stepped up to the border agent.

"You are English, Mr. Hubbard?" the official asked.

"Yes. From York," Adam replied with convincing British enunciation.

The agent looked down at a printout of a pair of photos, clearly visible on the countertop. One was of the pitted face of Nicholas Page when he was without a beard and had kept his hair cropped almost to his scalp. The other was an undergraduate pilot training class picture of the young lieutenant Tom Mercomes. The nose Adam had broken playing high school football still had a visible tilt to the right, his chin was narrower and without a cleft, and Mercomes had a distinctive receding hairline. Adam forced his jaw to relax and gazed pleasantly at the officer. The agent look steadily back, then at the two men who stood close behind him.

"Are you three together?"

"Yes. All traveling together."

"Where will you be staying?"

"Etosha Aoba Lodge in the park, like those ahead of us," Adam replied calmly.

"And the purpose of your visit to Namibia?"

"We are part of a multinational team assisting with a rhino count. I imagine some of our colleagues have already passed through."

"And why are you entering from Angola? I understood rhinos to be extinct in Angola since the war."

Adam nodded. "Unfortunately, that was the case. There is an effort to reintroduce them to Iona National Park. We have been evaluating their success." He wagged his head uncertainly. "So far, it is hard to judge how they will do."

The agent studied his face again, returned to the pair of photos, then hammered a stamp across the Namibian visa Dreu had inserted into the passport.

"Welcome to Namibia, Mr. Hubbard," he said. "Best of luck with your work here." Manny and Nick received a pleasant nod and a quick, authoritative drumming of his stamp.

"Well done," Nick said with a chuckle as they returned to the Ford. "Just goes to show what a little on-the-fly research can do. How did you know they were reintroducing rhinos to that Angolan park?"

"I didn't," Adam admitted. "But if they aren't, they should be. And I guessed he wouldn't know."

It was Adam's turn behind the wheel while Manny slept and Nick checked back with Ajani Botha whom he had called four hours earlier with his proposition. The searing heat of the afternoon sun shimmered off the flat ribbon of highway that stretched south into Namibia, turning the two paved lanes and treeless plain ahead into a mirage of liquid silver. The Ford's air conditioner had never been recharged and labored to seep tepid air across the three men. Adam cracked two windows to add a breeze.

"Ajani, you old pirate," Nick yelled into the phone, seemingly oblivious to the man stretched across the rear seat with an arm pressed tightly over his ear. "Have we tempted you with our offer?"

Nick nodded, his bearded chin tightening into a satisfied smirk as the South African replied with some insult of his own before agreeing to their terms.

"Alright, then," Nick shouted. "Send account information to the woman who contacted you. She will wire the first $100,000. The rest will be sent within minutes of the time we touch down in Europe. Where should we meet you in Windhoek?"

He turned to Adam and repeated the instructions as they were given. "Hosea Kutako International Airport. About forty-five kilometers east of the city. The smaller terminal handles domestic and freight carriers. You will meet us there and have clearances for us." He listened silently for a moment, his face relaxing into a sly grin, then said to Adam. "He says that may cost us another thousand apiece."

"Well worth it," Adam said with a nod. "Tell him we will call when we're an hour out. We'll want to get in the air immediately."

35

One thing was now clear to Amanda Nguyen. The man with Nick Page, the mysterious Mr. Solomon, had been sent by Unit 1. And she would bet her future with the Agency that it was Tom Mercomes.

Mercomes' history, what little of it remained, had been so difficult to uncover that she was certain he had disappeared into Unit 1. The few bits of information she was able to uncover convinced her he must be the elusive Mr. Solomon, the man Nicholas Page called Cyclops. She had initiated her search by working her way backward through Page's history, reviewing the series of fruitless attempts to locate the deserter since he had disappeared from Syria, then tracing the path that had taken him there as a CIA covert officer.

It was while reviewing Page's records as an Air Force flight instructor that she found reference to his having assisted another pilot safely to the ground whose canopy had been shattered by a bird strike during a two-ship, cross-country training flight to Enid, Oklahoma. Page had flown the approach and landing off the crippled aircraft's wing, giving the injured pilot, barely able to see through the blood and broken plexiglass, verbal instruction right to touchdown. The damaged plane carried the body of a student pilot who had been in the T-38's front seat and had taken the brunt of the direct hit. Both instructor pilots had been decorated. There was no mention in Page's record of the name of the man flying the crippled aircraft.

Amanda scoured through digital records of the Del Rio, Texas *News-Herald* where the flyers had been stationed at Laughlin Air Force Base, looking for details of the accident. Papers for the day of the incident and the following day were conveniently missing.

The same proved to be true of the Enid paper, the *News and Eagle*. Someone with exceptional hacking skills had entered the papers' digital files and deleted all issues Amanda guessed had listed a name that was not to be remembered. The same proved to be true of the Texas and Oklahoma state library archives.

On a hunch, she found the name of a student pilot at Laughlin who had been cited in an issue of the *News-Herald* for a traffic ticket two weeks following the accident. She brought up a record of the man's military service, traced him to a current address and phone number in Madison, Wisconsin, and cold called. She introduced herself as a reporter for *The Air Force Times*, doing an article on heroic saves following inflight accidents.

"I understand you were training at Laughlin when a student was killed by a bird strike and the pilot landed the plane," she began. "I wondered what you remembered about the accident?"

"Yes," the man said. "That was in the class ahead of mine. It was quite the big deal at the time."

"Hmm," Amanda murmured. "That's interesting. I can't find anything about it in the local paper around the time of the accident."

"That's strange. I remember a writeup. I think the student was from Ohio. His family came out to meet with the instructor and take the body home. The IP lost an eye. I think they moved him into a teaching position at the Academy."

"IP?" Amanda asked.

"Yeah. Sorry. The instructor pilot. Lieutenant Mercomes. He and the pilot who helped guide him down were decorated at a big ceremony on base before he left."

"Do you recall the other pilot's name?"

"Sure. Everyone was talking about them both. It was Captain Page."

"Thank you," Amanda said. "I'll see if I can track either of them down."

She ran a file check of Air Force Academy records for the name

Mercomes and found that a Captain Mercomes had been awarded an Instructor of the Year award, but had resigned his commission the following year at the end of his five-year military commitment. Then he disappeared. The pilot who owed Nicholas Page his life had lost sight in one eye. Cyclops.

The exchange with Dreu Sason in which she had thrown out Mercomes' name—and she was now convinced she was sparring with the fabled Dreu Sason—had eaten at her during the hours since. The woman's comment played over and over in her head like a pesky tune she couldn't shake. *"Nick Page is not the only person aware of the Syria debacle. What he knows, others know. And they have the best interests of the nation at heart. We would all be much better served if you left him alone."*

She knew from Page's file that he had been undercover in Syria, known as a loner who had "gone native" in the vernacular of the Agency to the point that everyone around him thought he was Syrian. The file indicated he had abandoned his post without notice and disappeared, taking with him secrets that were of enough importance to the CIA that they wanted him found and brought in. Nothing in the digital folder hinted at the secrets.

"The Syria debacle," Sason had called it. Amanda turned her attention to internal correspondence surrounding the Middle Eastern country's civil war in 2011, the year Page disappeared, searching for the clandestine officer's name. It appeared in a string of classified memos exchanged in late March of that year between the Director of Central Intelligence and the Director of Clandestine Operations. She scrolled slowly down through the chain of messages, occasionally casting a watchful eye toward the opening of her cubicle to see that she wasn't being observed.

D-CO: *Be aware we are getting pushback from Page on the Syria assignment. He believes removing Homsi will not have desired effect.*

DCI   *What's his beef?*

D-CO   *He is convinced Syria's current leadership is best for the country and for the US in the long term. Thinks BAA is genuinely interested in creating a secular state that, by ME standards, would be reasonably open. Opposition such as Homsi has sectarian agenda not friendly to our interests.*

DCI   *Then why not complete the assignment and remove Homsi?*

D-CO   *He knows that will do just what we intend it to do—fuel unrest and lead to civil war. He also believes it won't succeed. Page is convinced Russia and Iran will intervene to support BAA. Result will be long, deadly, and destructive, and BAA will not be removed. In his words, "This is one of the stupidest, half-assed ideas I've heard concerning the current situation." He thinks we should pressure BAA to get army to back off on protestors, restore calm, and avoid more bloodshed.*

DCI   *Not what our major ally in the region wants. They want BAA gone.*

D-CO   *Page is aware of that. Thinks we are foolish to let them drive policy that will add to instability and not produce desired result. Says we need to "Show we have some balls for a change."*

DCI   *He's forgetting who he works for—and the oath he took as an officer.*

D-CO   *He believes his oath to defend and protect doesn't support this order. And no one here really knows that country like Page does.*

DCI   *You tell him to do what he's told, or we'll get someone else to do the job. This is bigger than the three of us.*

D-CO   *Yes, Sir. I will convey that.*

DCI   *You do that. And tell him it needs to happen NOW!*

Amanda scanned messages for the next twenty-four hours, finding nothing. Then, another briefer exchange:

DCI   *I haven't seen anything concerning Homsi. What's happened?*

D-CO   *We've lost contact with Page, Sir. Nothing since I sent our reply.*

DCI   *Do you think he's bolted?*

D-CO   *I'm not sure, Sir. There's a chance.*

DCI   *Then get someone else in there to do the job. And find the SOB!*

Amanda cleared her screen and pushed back from the computer. So the Agency's best-informed source in Syria had advised senior people to back off on Bashar Al-Assad and convince him to make peace with the rebels. If they didn't, Russia and Iran might come in on the Syrian government's side, there would be a protracted civil war, and Assad would not be removed. Just what had happened, and not what the American public would like to hear!

"What he knows, others know," Dreu Sason had said concerning Page. *"And they have the best interests of the nation at heart."*

Amanda glanced again at the opening to her cubicle, feeling some of the surge of excitement that had accompanied her special assignment begin to ebb. She had become the knot in the rope in a tug-of-war between the director and a unit over which he had lost control, and she was beginning to wonder in which direction she wanted to be pulled. It had been drummed into her head that the Agency's mission was to "collect, analyze, evaluate, and disseminate foreign intelligence to assist the President and senior US government policymakers in making decisions relating to national security." But she had never taken the time to consider what that responsibility was if she considered those decisions to be poorly conceived or just plain wrong. And from what little she had learned about Unit 1, part of its job was to clean up messes when that turned out to be the case. Dreu Sason was telling her she might be in the middle of one of those messes.

As she sat stewing over the dilemma, the screen attached to the computer to her left that was programmed to watch for new data related to the case flashed a warning. The identifier box beside it said "Nicholas Page." She leaned forward and clicked on the link. It opened and decrypted a message to the Director of Covert Operations from the CIA's Chief-of-Station, Johannesburg, South Africa.

Re your "All-Stations" alert concerning Nicholas Page. We and South African intelligence routinely monitor the phone of high profile South African smuggler, forger, and enabler named Ajani Botha. He has just arranged to fly to Namibia (Hosea Kutako International Airport), to pick up a passenger we suspect to be Page. SA Intel has notified Zambian and Namibian State Police. Namibia registered three Caucasian men entering from Angola at 13:37 hours today. Bearded man (photo

*attached) may be Page. Zambia flying SWAT team over from
Livingston. Awaiting instructions.*

She quickly entered a command to direct the program to follow
the chain of activity generated by the message. It showed an
immediate forward to the director's office. For the five minutes
that followed, there was nothing. Then, a message back to the
Director of Covert Operations instructing him to gather a list of all
assets in and within two hours of Windhoek, Namibia and bring it
personally to the director's desk. Share the South African
communique with no one. They were going after Page.

Amanda closed her eyes and tilted her chin upward. *"We would
all be much better served if you left him alone,"* the Unit 1 people
had advised. Who was "We?" Had Dreu meant the Unit 1 people?
The Agency in general? Everyone in the country? If it was
everyone, where did her knowing about it, and about the plan
underway to intercept Page in Namibia, fit into her responsibilities
as a national security officer and into the grand scheme of things?

She pushed away from her desk, left her cubicle, and walked to
the water cooler and coffee machine beside the door into the cyber
operations area. She poured a cup of coffee, realized she really
didn't want it this late in the day, and emptied it into the sink
beside the coffeemaker. What difference did it make, ten years
after the fact, that US intelligence had been given sound advice
about the adverse consequences of a single decision in Syria and
chose to ignore it? A decade of civil war and tens of thousands of
dead and displaced Syrians might be a reason. That damage
couldn't be undone. But the future of the man who had refused to
carry out the action item that was part of the decision? That was
still being determined. Could what she was considering be
treasonous? How could it be, if it was going to a unit created by
the Agency? Especially if she didn't share anything classified.

She filled a cup with water, carried it back to her station, and
stared at her screens for long enough she worried someone might

stick a head in to see why they heard no activity. Then she scooted her chair forward, tapped her computer back to life, and launched a brief encrypted message to a site she felt confident Dreu Sason would be monitoring.

Look at today's DCI exchanges.

36

The younger of the two CIA men had come to the room to tell them they were free to leave—the black agent who wasn't nearly as full of himself as that Pollard. He had simply said that she and Wes could go and thanked them for their information. No "Best of luck" or "Be careful out there." Just "Thanks for your help. You are both free to go."

The couple had spent their two days of confinement haunting the hotel gift shop and the stands of nearby street vendors for native souvenirs: masks, feathered rattles, carved bowls, and figurines that, when wrapped in heavy paper and packed tightly around four human bone fragments, made the lot look like common tourist trinkets. They wandered far enough from the hotel to find a TNT Express parcel outlet and shipped the box to Wesley's Providence apartment. Then they waited for their release.

Wes had purchased open-ended return fares to New York on Lufthansa. Twenty minutes in the hotel's business office secured them two seats on a flight leaving Luanda at 18:35 that evening. They left the Hotel International without checking again with the agents, reaching Quatro de Fevereiro's transcontinental terminal by taxi two-and-a-half hours before flight time. As Taylor led Wesley toward the Lufthansa check-in counter, two beret-capped officers in the charcoal gray uniforms of the Angolan National Police moved quickly from a perch beside one of the terminal's front windows and intercepted the couple. Both had AK-47s strapped around their shoulders.

"Good afternoon, Miss Dennis," one of the men said politely. "Would you both come with us, please?"

Taylor paled and looked desperately to Wes but found him

frantically searching the terminal as if looking for an escape.

"What's the problem, Officer?" she stammered, fishing in the pocket of her shoulder bag. "I think you must have me mistaken for someone else. My name is Linda Griffith, and I'm Canadian."

The officer smiled broadly. "I don't recall that we mentioned nationality, Miss Dennis. And your friend here? Is he also Canadian?"

She glanced again at Wesley who had folded into a resigned slump.

"Please follow me," the officer said. "We do not wish to draw attention here in the terminal area." He started toward one of the nondescript doors that opened into the rooms behind the counters. The second officer moved behind them to follow.

In a small, windowless room somewhere in the bowels of the baggage area they were seated at a plain wooden table.

"We will need to search your bags," the lead officer said, taking the two carry-ons without permission and handing them to the second man, who opened them in front of the couple and roughly spread the contents across the tabletop. He sorted through the piles of clothing and toiletries, then shrugged at his partner, muttering something Taylor couldn't understand.

"And where are the things you took from Zambia?" the lead officer asked.

She glared at him defiantly. "As you can see, I didn't take anything. This is all we have. I was plane-wrecked out in the bush two weeks ago, and had to hike out. Most of this I bought when I got back to civilization. Ask those two CIA guys who ratted on us."

The Angolan officer arched a brow. "CIA guys? We have been watching for you and Mr. Hylton since your plane was found in Angolan territory. And here you both are."

Wesley straightened in his chair. "I am *not* Matt Hylton," he said urgently, fishing out his own passport. "My name is Wesley Epling. I flew here to meet Taylor and have been waiting here in

Luanda for the past two weeks."

Taylor cast him a withering glare. "You pathetic little worm," she hissed. The officer drew a piece of paper from his shirt pocket, studied what she guessed from the rear shadow of the print to be a photo of the anthropology team standing beside the Kodiak, then gave a surprised nod.

"It appears that you are *not* Mr. Hylton," he agreed. "But you will still need to come with us to our headquarters in the city until we learn what you have done with the relics Miss Dennis took from Zambia."

"As I told you," Taylor said sharply. "This is all we have. And you are going to make us late for our flight."

The officer held up her Canadian passport. "It appears that you were planning to leave using false documents. That is a violation of our law as well as theft. I think we will need to keep both of you here until the Zambian authorities arrive. I suspect they will have no claim on you, Mr. Epling. But you will stay until we know for certain. Perhaps you were here to assist with a theft."

"I just came to meet my fiancée on her way home from Africa," Epling pleaded. "I had nothing to do with any theft."

"You complete shit-faced worm!" Taylor snarled.

37

His two days in Huambo had also been used by the Sicilian to good advantage. The city that filled the dubious role of having been the center of the Angolan civil war still supported a flourishing black market in arms and ammunition. He had little trouble finding a Finnish-made Tikka T3x TAC A1 sniper's rifle, what he considered to be the premier weapon for long-range accuracy. And it broke down conveniently into a case that could just as easily have carried expensive fishing gear.

His purchase included fifty rounds of ammunition. North of the city, he found an isolated stretch of empty land behind a rock formation the size of a sports arena where he could sight and finetune the weapon at different distances. He then called three charter services at the Huambo airport until he found one that had an aircraft with the range he might require, planes readily available on short notice, and willingness to fly across international borders.

He was seated at lunch when his phone buzzed with a message from Magnum44.

Page and two male companions in Namibia. Rendezvous planned at Windhoek International Airport around 21:00 hours. Pickup flight is an Embraer 600 from Johannesburg with large black B on tail.

He glanced at his watch. It was 13:00. He had eight hours.

He was airborne within sixty minutes, the lone passenger on a Gulfstream GV, leased for two days for $14,000. He wore a charcoal gray business suit, starched white shirt, and conservative tie. His only luggage was a thin suit bag and a worn leather case. Inflight, he studied a terminal map of Hosea Kutako International, identified strategic firing locations depending on where the aircraft parked, and determined that a rental car might allow better positioning. By the time he touched down at 16:30, a navy blue Nissan Altima was waiting.

"If I finish my business, I may want to return to Huambo late tonight," he told the charter pilot as he disembarked. "Can you have the plane fueled and ready to leave if I give you a call? I'll know by 22:00."

"Yes, Sir. We can be ready," the captain agreed.

The man from Taormina paused at the top of the fold-down steps. "I'm surprised this airport is so far from the city," he said. "Isn't there a field closer to Windhoek?"

The pilot nodded. "The old airport. Windhoek Eros Airfield. It is right in the city."

The Sicilian steered the rented Nissan to the edge of airport parking, turned the air conditioning to full cool, and thought through the next five hours. Somehow, Magnum already knew Page was in Namibia and headed for a pickup in Windhoek. His target had been joined by another man, possibly two, who appeared to have access to the same sources of information. By now, or very soon, they would be aware that the Agency knew they were bound for the Namibian capital and expecting a pickup at Hosea Kutako. So—what would they do if both they and their rescue pilot were committed to a rendezvous in Windhoek, but suspected someone might be waiting?

He pulled up a map of the Windhoek area on his phone, traced the thirty-five kilometers of road that connected the city to the international airport, then started the Nissan and headed for the village of Hoffnung, midway in between.

38

Nick Page had no more than laid the satellite phone back in the cup holder between seats when it buzzed with a call from Dreu. Adam had not expected to hear from her until they were in the air and glanced down nervously. He snatched it up, quickly confirmed the incoming caller code, then hit the green answer button.

"Has something changed?" he asked urgently.

Her tone reflected the same concern. "Where is your incoming flight?"

"Nick just talked to him. He's about an hour out. What's up?"

"And where are you?"

"We're about an hour and a half away. Botha is planning to get on the ground, arrange for fuel, then do what he needs to do to get us around customs before we arrive."

Dreu's voice remained intense. "They know you're coming."

Adam glanced over at his seatmate, wondering if he had heard Dreu's warning. It was clear from the grim frown that he had.

"How the hell did they find out?" Adam demanded. "Did Botha turn on us?"

"No. I guess he's involved in enough shady stuff that we and South African Intel keep bugs on his phones. In fact, I looked him up in the system and found half a dozen references. They've been listening in on his conversations with Nick and know he's headed to Windhoek to meet him."

"How did you learn this? I thought they had gone silent on you."

"Someone inside tipped me off. I'm guessing our new acquaintance. The message from South Africa to Clandestine Ops came in through channels I could access and she directed me to it.

It was immediately forwarded to the director, and I caught their initial exchange before they went to face-to-face. They know Nick's got a beard and that the three of you are in Namibia. The director asked for a list of all Namibian assets."

"Shit," Adam swore. "Do you think the phone Botha has with him in the air is being monitored?"

"I wouldn't be surprised. Don't count on secure calls."

Adam looked again at Nick who gave him a quick, frowning nod. "Thanks, Base," Adam said. "We'll take it from here. Back with you when a solution is in place."

"Be careful," she pleaded.

Manny had twisted upright behind them and leaned forward over the center console. "I heard most of that," he said. "Sounds like someone's going to be waiting for us."

Adam grunted his displeasure. "They are if our ride lands in Windhoek. Nick, does he have anyone with him?"

The bearded man shrugged. "I didn't ask him. He's flying an E-600 and we're looking at some long legs. I'd guess he's got a second pilot."

"Call him again and see if there is someone else with a phone. He has this number. Get him to call us from another cell. Manny, check other airports around Windhoek that can take an Embraer 600—runways of at least 1500 meters."

Nick quickly made the contact, conveyed the message, and nodded to the others that Botha had a copilot. Within a minute, they had a return call.

"Hey, partner. American CIA and South African Intelligence are monitoring your calls," Nick informed him. "They know you are coming to pick us up. We need you to divert."

"Windhoek Eros Airport," Manny called from the center seat. "Five miles south of the city center."

Nick repeated the suggestion, then listened intently. "Roger that," he said and clicked off the phone.

"He knows Eros and said he has taken the plane in there before.

He'll call to divert as late as he can, but still needs fuel. Even if they don't know he diverted until he's on the ground, he figures he'll need to be down for thirty minutes, minimum. He advised that we park in the lot just below the control tower and come through the door farthest to the right. He'll meet us in the hallway. But if people at the international airport are monitoring his radio transmissions and hustle, they may be able to get to Eros before we can get back in the air."

Adam glanced in his mirrors and eased the Ford up to 120 kilometers per hour. "We'll just have to take that chance," he muttered.

The main parking area at Windhoek Eros was nearly full, but the side lot in front of the tower held only three vehicles. Adam wheeled the Expedition into the spot closest to the door Botha had described, and the three men grabbed their backpacks. The hunting rifles remained on the floor in front of the rear seat.

The Afrikaner who met them in the hallway was a giant of a man, an inch or two taller than Adam and thirty pounds heavier, with powerful shoulders that seemed to span the narrow corridor. His hair was shaved to the scalp on the sides with a flat top above a square jaw. A short, thickly muscled neck gave his head the appearance of springing directly from those massive shoulders. He clasped hands with Nick as though they had met this way a dozen times, then turned without speaking and led toward the back of the building.

"Any signs of trouble?" Nick asked after him.

Botha's head shake turned his whole upper body. "I waited to divert until ten minutes out. Told them my cargo had been delivered to the wrong airport. There is no traffic up there right now, so no delays getting down. The field had a fuel truck waiting, and one of my mates here was happy to pass you on through for a contribution to his kids' school fund. We should be able to board and leave."

He guided them through the door at the end of the hallway onto a concrete apron. The Embraer idled fifty meters from the building, its door-mounted stairway extended to the ramp. Botha walked confidently toward the waiting aircraft with the three men following, Adam chatting with Nick and Manny about the short-field capabilities of the E-600 as if this were any casual departure. Botha mounted the steps two at a time. Manny followed, his shorter legs needing each tread. Adam waved Nick ahead, but his old wingman deferred. Adam scrambled up the aluminum steps, paused briefly at the top to give the field around them a quick scan, then froze in place. Behind a gate in an eight-meter chain link fence, a dark sedan had pulled up tightly against the steel mesh. A figure in a dark hoodie leaned through the open driver's window, chin pressed tight against the stock of a silenced rifle that extended through the links.

Adam ducked instinctively, reaching toward Nick who was two steps from the doorway.

"Nick!" he hissed lowly, but the sound didn't reach his friend before the bullet ripped into his skull, throwing him left over the silver railing.

"Nick!" Adam shouted as a vice-like hand gripped his arm and jerked him into the aircraft cabin.

"*Go!*" Botha screamed at the man in the cockpit's right seat, yanking up the stairs and slamming the plane's door into place. He threw down the lock lever as the engines screamed, twisting the fuselage away from the fallen man. "*Don't wait to be cleared! Get us in the air!*" Botha shouted.

Adam scrambled back to the first window, glanced quickly toward the gate where the sedan had already disappeared, then watched as the left engine swept over the lifeless body of the man he had come to rescue.

39

Amanda Nguyen re-read the one-line message from the South African desk, then slowly sorted through it again.

Page situation resolved. Two companions left with Botha by air. Destination unknown.

Page situation resolved. Did that mean they had captured him? The message said "two companions." Was someone other than Mercomes with him? And had they been allowed to leave? Or had they somehow escaped while Page was detained? She was certain Dreu Sason would be monitoring messages coming in from Africa and seemed to have all the tools she needed to decode them. She would see the dispatch. And Amanda wanted so badly to talk to her about it.

Would they bring Page back to Washington? She was certain that most of the cyber-operations analysts knew about black sites outside of the United States where the Agency held and questioned enemy combatants. Her single year intercepting and analyzing data had exposed her to secret locations in Poland and Romania where captives were imprisoned and subjected to "advanced interrogation" techniques. Would that be Page's fate? It was clear the Agency didn't want him in a position to go public with what he knew about early Syrian developments. But how were they ever going to convince him to keep quiet when he'd worked so hard to evade them for nearly a decade?

And what about the men who had "left with Botha?" Either the people who had intercepted Page hadn't been interested in them, or the notorious Botha had managed to get them aboard and into the air. If that were the case, where could they possibly go that they couldn't be tracked and picked up?

Amanda turned to the computer that watched for Sason's intrusions into the system. And there she was. Though it had only been moments since the Africa message arrived, the Unit's cyber expert had entered for a look. She must have a program that continuously scanned internal communication for anything remotely related to their operations and flagged her the second something appeared. Amanda waited breathlessly. Within two minutes a message appeared that sent her mind reeling.

You killed him, you idiots! What ever happened to "defend and protect?" Damn you all!

40

As Botha's co-pilot swung the nose of the Embraer toward the short taxiway that led to the end of Runway 19, Adam's rage had risen with the scream of the twin engines. His first impulse had been to shout for Botha to return, to swing back to pick up the fallen man. But he realized any hesitation would lead to them all being arrested and imprisoned, to questions he had no intention of answering, and to many he did not have answers to. And he understood that the methods used to extract that information would be harsh and painful. He also doubted his own embassy would give aid to an invisible man who had entered Namibia on a British passport, one the CIA would want to talk to as desperately as the Namibian authorities. But he had failed Nick in the worst possible way. Led him into a trap that Adam's involvement had likely created.

He had scrambled back across the cabin to the windows on the right, watching an emergency crew race toward a ramp-side fire station where a wide door swept rapidly upward. They were going to try to intercept the aircraft. To position a truck across the runway before the plane could get into the air. But Botha had thrown himself into his seat, taken over the controls, and forced the nimble jet at a dangerous speed through a screeching turn onto the airstrip's centerline. The throttles had reached full takeoff position before he had even straightened into the roll. Adam had dropped into the nearest seat, clipped his seatbelt across his lap, and craned to peer at the desperate fire team as they ended their sprint, realizing they could not stop the speeding jet.

As the plane lifted off, he had looked beyond the buildings for the dark sedan. It could have been any of a dozen now parked in the airport lot or moving along the access road into the city. He struggled to remember the shooter. The hooded head had been pressed tightly behind a powerful scope, the gloved hands on the stalk and trigger grip hiding most of the face. Had the shooter been white or black? He couldn't be sure. He suddenly remembered that he wasn't alone in the cabin.

The plane's interior was customized into two sections. In the front, a shortened passenger cabin held two pair of plush seats facing each other across a mahogany table on one side of the aisle, and three singles facing forward on the other. The rear two-thirds of the cabin, accessible through a door in the back of the passenger area, was outfitted for cargo. Manny Beg had thrown himself in the last of the single seats. When Adam turned, he found his agent staring grimly down at the receding suburbs of Windhoek.

"Are you alright, Manny?" he asked. "I only heard one shot."

"I'd made it inside," Manny muttered. "Do you think they just wanted Nick?"

Adam pushed from his seat and took one across the aisle from Manny. "My guess is yes. I saw the shooter just as Nick was hit. He was in a car behind a chain link gate beside the building we came through. He could have hit any of us, but probably knew he would only get one shot."

"And he didn't make any effort to cripple the plane," Manny added. "A couple of shots into an engine would have kept us on the ground. I've been thinking he wanted the rest of us to get away."

Adam nodded. "If we were arrested and talked, we could point fingers. And if we're gone, we're unlikely to talk to anyone."

"Exactly," Manny agreed. "Could you see the shooter?"

Adam gave him a dubious shake of the head. "Not well. I was just thinking about that. Hood pulled over his forehead. Looking through a scope. Gloved hands. I can't even guess at color—or, for that matter, sex. It could have been a woman."

"Want to guess at who?" Manny asked.

Adam shook his head. "Three possibilities that I can think of.

We know the Agency's been after him. They may have decided this was the best way to keep him quiet. Dreu said Zambia was bringing a team in from Livingston. But they would have been coming by air into the other airport. And if they'd somehow managed to get to Eros before us, they could have intercepted us when we came out of the building."

"Unless they didn't want to mess with extradition," Manny suggested. "I don't know what the relationship is like between these countries."

"Yes, but for a theft of a couple of bones? I don't think so."

Manny nodded. "What's three?"

Adam twisted in the chair so he could look more directly at the agent. "We told you enough when you joined us that you know why Nick left Syria. The mission he refused to carry out was completed by someone else. Nick had tipped off the rebels that there might be an attempt on a man named Homsi, and they were ready for him. Not ready enough to keep Homsi from being killed, but they captured the shooter within minutes. I guess they tortured the guy pretty brutally before he was swapped in a prisoner exchange. Just before you picked us up, Nick told me this guy blamed him for the capture and torture, and became obsessed with getting back at him. The guy's been trying to get to him as long as the Agency has, and has come closer."

Manny frowned skeptically. "How would he have known we were going to be at Windhoek? Especially at Eros?"

"Nick seemed fairly certain the man was being fed information from inside, maybe with the hope he would get to Nick and save the Agency the trouble. He seemed to have been hovering close by for a long time." Adam paused, then confessed, "and I think he may have followed me from Zambia. I may have led him right to Nick."

"Bullshit," Manny scoffed. "I don't know how, but someone inside obviously knew we were going to be in Windhoek in time to intercept."

Adam shook his head bitterly. "They knew because I told a driver in Zambia that I was headed west. Going to Zambezi. That shifted their whole search in this direction."

"So you think you're the only sonofabitch who was smart enough to figure that out? Give me a break. You may have been a day ahead, but I'd guess that with you or not, sooner or later Nick was going to call Botha. The only reason we came close to getting out was because your woman in the Unit learned they were tapping Botha's calls. Otherwise, they'd have had him trapped out at the international airport. Hell, by diverting Botha to Eros, you almost got him out!"

"Almost isn't good enough," Adam muttered.

Manny sniffed. "In this business, sometimes that's all we're lucky enough to get. So quit beating yourself up and realize you did one helluva job. Now—where do you think we're headed?"

After a steep turn to the west, Adam had felt the plane level at what he guessed to be about five thousand feet above the ground, then begin a gradual descent until near a thousand. Ground-heated air bounced and rocked the aircraft as he rose and navigated his way to the cockpit, pushing open the unlatched door. "Do we have a destination?" he shouted through the covering of Botha's headphones.

The massive South African had the autopilot off and handled the yoke like a man guiding a luxury sedan over a rutted gravel road. He replied without looking back at his passenger.

"I'm going to stay low. I don't believe they will scramble any of their air force to intercept a plane that left without clearance, but I'm not taking any chances. One base in Namibia is within a hundred miles of the route I want to take, so I plan to stay out of sight. At this altitude, with the equipment they have out in this part of the country, they shouldn't be able to track us. We will make one fuel stop in Northern Chad."

"Chad?"

"Yes. In what they call the Aouzou Strip. Nothing but sand for miles in any direction. Hot as hell. But a safe refueling stop."

"What's our final destination?"

"I haven't firmed up anything beyond Chad," Botha confessed. "We are working on that now. Before we became fugitives, I had us flight-planned into Amsterdam. We won't want to go there now, but should be able to get into one of the Balkan countries where they don't worry too much about where we have come from. We can reach that part of Europe from Chad without another stop. If I am not able to reach my contacts there, we may be stuck out in that desert."

"Wonderful," Adam said with a scowl.

"Not to worry," Botha shouted with a reassuring jerk of the head. "I know good people in Albania." He looked back at Adam for the first time. "I am very sorry about Nick," he muttered. "He was a good man. He has been running for a long time."

Adam nodded soberly. "Yes, he has. And he was looking for a way out. But not that way." He backed cautiously out of the cockpit, bracing himself against the jarring turbulence as he made his way back to his seat.

"Next stop, Chad," he muttered to Manny as he dropped into the chair and punched in the call to Dreu Sason with the news about Nick that had triggered her bitter message to Amanda Nguyen. "It's going to be one hell of a rough ride, I'm afraid."

41

Marshall Pollard pulled the mask more tightly down over his chin and grimaced at the stench of death that still seeped through the cloth covering. He stood across a stainless steel table from Justin Turnley who was buttoning the front of his jacket against the chill of the dank air that filled the morgue. Both stared down at the corpse of former CIA clandestine ops officer Nicholas Page. The body had not been autopsied, but lay naked on the metal surface, a white towel draped across the groin.

"Are you confident enough to make a definite ID?" Turnley asked, turning slightly to look more directly at the bearded face that had largely been spared as the bullet removed much of the back of the skull.

"We never met, but I'm pretty certain," Pollard said with enough hesitation that Turnley's grim expression deepened. "He's got the pocked face and, without the beard, would look like the guy in the team photo at the Kabwe dig. Unless that man wasn't the right guy, I think we have Page."

Pollard waved for a white-smocked attendant to hand him a flat ink pad, took the hand of the deceased that lay nearest him, and rolled the thumb and middle finger across the square. The attendant replaced the pad with a white card with five labeled boxes and watched curiously as the American agent pressed the stained digits into the first and center spots.

"I'll photograph these and send them to Langley," Pollard muttered. "They have his prints. That will give us confirmation."

Turnley took a step back from the table, scowling beneath his mask at the sight of the damaged head. "Who do you think did this?" he asked the older agent. "Is this what happens when you know some company secrets and get crosswise with the Agency?"

Pollard waved the card in the dank air to dry the prints, then turned toward the door. "Hell, we all know about some of the screwups," he said cynically. "But Page did more than just get crosswise with the powers that be. He basically deserted his post in the middle of an international security crisis."

Turnley sniffed loudly. "Whose crisis? I don't know that the US was at risk. Does this mean we can't just walk away from something we don't think is right?"

"Resigning is one thing," Pollard argued, pushing out into a basement hallway that smelled more of disinfectant than death. "Walking away without telling anyone is another. Page deserted. Like going AWOL while in combat. And, as I said, I doubt Langley sanctioned this hit."

Turnley shook his head skeptically. "You saw the directive asking for a list of all assets in the region. We're here. No one else connected to the Agency is here that we know of. But who else knew Page was coming?"

Pollard laid the card with the dead man's prints on a rolling gurney tucked against a sidewall and pulled out his phone. "The people who were helping Page knew. So it's hard to say how many others. It seemed to be a pretty open secret. And we know Zambia was sending in a special ops team. That doesn't sound like a standard response to going after someone who *might* have assisted with a theft. Maybe he was involved with this Botha guy in some ways we don't know about." He snapped four pictures of the prints, changing distance and angle. "We suspect the Zambians beat us here, and we haven't seen any sign of them. Why would they disappear?"

"Maybe because the man they came to arrest was shot down at a public airport," Turnley countered. "I think I'd be quietly getting the hell back across the border too."

Pollard headed for the stairs at the end of the corridor. "Let's get up where I can get a better signal and I'll send these prints. Then I think we might want to do the same."

Turnley stopped and looked back toward the door to the morgue. "What about Page's body?"

Pollard kept walking. "I told the guy back there to hang onto it until he hears from us. Someone at the Agency can tell them what they want done with it. Our assignment was to find the man. If the prints match, we've done our job."

"Pretty sorry way to end a career he thought was one of service to country," Turnley muttered.

The door opened onto a quiet side street lined by high, whitewashed walls. The men turned toward a wider boulevard where light traffic passed the police station along lanes divided by a row of expertly trimmed palms. Pollard paused, checked his signal strength, then entered a quick message and sent the prints into cyberspace. Turnley had moved ahead, unlocking the doors of a rented Corolla. He slid into the driver's seat and when Pollard joined him, guided the Toyota into traffic and headed back toward the international airport. With the body on the slab, their break from the hum-drum of routine intelligence work appeared to have come to an end.

42

The message from Amanda Nguyen struck Dreu as personal.

I am so sorry, Dreu. I had no idea this was going to happen. I am not sure we were to blame, at least not directly. Messages from the field sound surprised. Officer Turnley, Chief of Station in Botswana, demanded to know if we were responsible. Nothing coming from the DCI's office.

Be forewarned. I meet each morning to brief the DCI on what I have learned about Unit 1. I feel a responsibility to do this job as ordered and report my findings. I will be telling the director I believe you and Tom Mercomes are part of Unit 1. I have already shared a photo of Mercomes from one of the pilot training yearbooks. The director has given no further indication of what he plans to do with the information but has asked that I try to determine who else is working with you. Since three men crossed into Namibia, I am assuming two of your people went to rescue Page. We have requested passport photos from the Namibian government. I should have them within the day. I have seen no indication the Agency is trying to track the plane that left Windhoek. Everything has gone silent internally. Be aware.

Dreu studied the message, wondering how much trust to put in this woman who seemed suddenly to have become a co-conspirator. Had she asked if Dreu knew where Adam and Manny were headed, Dreu would have been fully suspicious. By not asking, was she showing that she wasn't trying to probe, hoping

Dreu might accept her as an ally and volunteer information their internal sources couldn't dig up? She felt like a caller who, as seconds passed, knew her phone was being traced. Her gut screamed *Cut this woman off!* Her analyst's mind said, *Test her a little and see what you can learn from her.* She replied:

An expression of concern from Turnley and no reply from the director? I'd say silence speaks volumes. What happened to Page's body? And what can you tell me about Severu Messina? That file seems to have been buried deeper than I can reach.

The reply was immediate.

As I said, all silent internally about Windhoek. Will look into Messina.

The satphone buzzed beside her on the desk. She quickly closed the access portal into the Agency files and snatched up the handset.

"Tell me you're safe," she begged.

"So far, all clear," he answered. "We have a fuel stop to make. Botha believes he's found a place in Europe where he can drop us off safely. He's waiting confirmation. I won't be contacting you again until we're on the ground there or unless the drop falls through. Have you contacted the rest of the team and instructed them to get stateside?"

"Yes. Tony's on his way here from Korea. Britt needed another day to tidy up some things on the Venezuelan project. She should be starting back early tomorrow."

"What are you hearing from your new friend in Cyber Ops?"

"We just exchanged messages. She doesn't seem to believe the Agency sanctioned Page's death. Apparently, one of the officers who's been tracking him sent a message asking if it was a Company hit. They've been silent inside, but she hasn't seen any indication the order came from Langley." Dreu paused, then added, "She's systematically working her way into our ranks, Adam. She's ID'd me, and has a pretty good idea that Tom Mercomes came into the Unit and is Mr. Solomon—or Cyclops. They have your photos coming from Namibia, so they will probably be able to identify you and Manny."

"I thought we purged him from every record file he's been in," Adam protested.

"You thought you had been purged as Mercomes," she reminded him. "Somewhere, there is a record with Manny's picture, and this woman is good. I believe she'll find it."

"She told you all this?"

"She did. She obviously feels obligated to carry out the assignment she's been given, but also seems to feel a need to let us know where she is with her search. She's either probing me for information, or trying to keep us a step ahead of what she's telling the director. So far, I can't be sure which."

Adam sighed irritably. "Okay. I'm going to activate the tracking device on this phone. If in three days, I don't show up at the location I'm going to give you, initiate a track and send Britt and Tony to find us. But if all goes as planned, here's what I want you to do. . ."

43

"I just got confirmation," Ajani Botha said, steadying himself with a hand on the edge of the table against the constant chop created by the sweltering air rising from the naked dunes a thousand feet below. He threw himself loosely into the chair opposite Adam. "Korçë will let us in—no questions asked. Some of my associates will meet us there. If you would like to add another ten thousand to what I am being paid, they will take you to a place you can cross into Greece without having to show papers. It is a drive of about thirty kilometers. Not far. And a very safe crossing. Then you are on your own."

Adam nodded. "I'll call as soon as we're on the ground. The rest of your money can be transferred while we wait, including what you need for your friends."

Botha glanced at a large black digital watch. "We should be touching down in Chad in just under an hour. Half an hour to refuel, then another three to Korçë. There is nothing at this airstrip but a few buildings and sand. You may get off if you wish, but I recommend you stay on board and out of sight." He grinned over at Manny. "These strips are the haunts of profiteers like me. We don't want them to think our cargo may be more valuable to them than the king's ransom they charge me for fuel."

"I see no reason to get off," Adam agreed. "And we'll stay out of sight." Botha pushed up from the deep chair, gave them both a curt nod, and grasped the edge of the overhead bins as he sailor-walked his way back to the cockpit.

"Korçë?" Manny asked.

"Albania," Adam explained. "Not an EU country and still pretty loosely regulated. The city is in the south and has a large Greek population that's been at odds with the government since the country was formed. A good place to get onto the continent without questions. And Botha's friends will get us safely into Greece."

Manny smiled thinly. "For a price."

"Everything is for a price," Adam said grimly.

"Any information from the home office about who got to Nick?" Manny asked.

Adam gazed out the window at the featureless landscape below. "Apparently one of the men assigned to find him was surprised. So I don't think it was the pair who were following me. But the director had asked for a list of other CIA assets in the region. Maybe they called in someone else."

"What about this Severu Messina?"

Adam tilted his head skeptically. "Possible. But as much trouble as I had finding Nick—and I think I was able to get into his head about as well as anyone could—I don't see how Messina could have ended up in Windhoek at exactly that moment."

"Unless he was being fed information that was as good as yours," Manny suggested.

Adam sniffed. "They had two of their best guys in Africa trying to follow him, and they didn't get there in time." The plane began a gradual descent toward the desert below.

"Maybe someone wanted Messina there before the other agents," Manny muttered, staring out his own window at the endless wasteland.

The fuel stop was all Botha had promised: a seven-thousand foot strip of cracked concrete beside two mud brick buildings, fronted by an apron not much larger than the aircraft. Two battered fuel trucks left the open side of one of the makeshift hangars before the plane had fully come to a stop. They were escorted by a battle-worn Toyota Hilux carrying three men in desert camo and black berets, one standing behind an old Soviet DShK machinegun on a tripod.

Adam and Manny pulled back from the windows into the shadows of the cabin as Botha opened the main door and extended the fold-down stairs. Once he reached the pavement, they heard him shout instructions in French to the man driving the pickup, then clamber back up to sit on the top step.

"Who the hell are these guys?" Adam called up to him as the truck eased away to convey the order.

Botha grinned back at his passengers. "Carryovers from the Chad-Libyan war," he shouted. "I don't know which side they were on. This is still a contested strip of land. These men smuggle fuel down from Libya or over from the Sudan to operate this stop for people like me. It costs ten to twenty times standard rates. But then," he said with a light chuckle, "that is why we are here. We can't buy at standard rates."

"How many flights come through here a day?" Adam asked.

Botha shrugged. "Four or five. These men make a fortune. We are probably supporting some rebel group somewhere. Might be Boko Haram or Al-Shabaab for all I know." He chuckled. "In this part of the world, you never know for certain who you are helping and who you are fighting."

He pulled a small pair of binoculars from a pants pocket and watched gauges on the rear of the trucks as the uniformed men pumped fuel into the wings. When the pickup circled around again, he descended the steps, handed a small canvas bag through the window, and stepped away, remaining at the bottom of the stairs until the money was counted and a signal given that the smugglers were satisfied.

"You don't get back on the plane until the money is counted," he called back to them as he pulled the stairs back into place and sealed the door. "But there is an honor among thieves. Their fuel is always good, and they hold to their price." He gave Adam and Manny a quick salute. "And I am always good to my promises. Final leg. You should be in Greece in time for a late supper."

44

The director sat back with his left ankle crossed over his knee and a yellow legal pad balanced on his lap. Amanda faced him across his neatly arranged desk, sitting stiffly upright and feeling torn apart inside.

"We have compared the photo of Mercomes in the pilot training class yearbook to the passport picture of the man who crossed into Namibia as the Englishman, Daniel Hubbard," the director said, tapping his pen against the pad. "There has been some work done on the face. A straightened nose and a good job of transplanting hair. But our people believe it's the same man. Not positive, but eighty percent certain. And you are now certain this woman you asked about earlier is involved. This Dreu Sason."

Amanda swallowed nervously. "Yes, Sir. I believe Ms. Sason is their cyber-specialist." She briefly reviewed Dreu's credentials, her involvement in the case involving the Chinese children who had been called Weavers, and her unexplained disappearance. "I have made contact with her," she told the director, "and confronted her with the information I have. She neither confirms nor denies."

The director aggressively underlined an entry on his pad. "Is she good?" he asked.

Amanda gave a single quick nod. "Yes, Sir. She is very good."

He looked up from the pad with a slight smile. "As good as you?"

"Yes, Sir. I believe she is better than I am. I cannot determine how she enters the system, and she knows how to leave messages only I will find."

"Has she said anything about this African affair?"

Amanda hesitated, then ventured, "Yes, Sir. She believes we

killed someone named Nicholas Page."

The director *hmphed* under his breath and tapped again against the pad. "And what did you tell her?"

"I told her I had seen nothing that indicated we were involved."

"Good answer," he said with a curt nod. "What else has she had to say?"

"She told me that she believes the Unit's effectiveness depends on them remaining completely anonymous and independent. They are quite disturbed that we are trying to identify their members."

The director tossed the pad onto his desk and pushed farther back in his chair. "Of course they're disturbed. They want to do whatever they damn well please. But they work for us, damn it. Or, at least they're supposed to. But this is the second time they've stuck their little anonymous noses into something that was ours to handle."

Amanda thought he was expecting her to say something. Perhaps, "I understand, Sir." But she remained quiet. His face tightened into a thoughtful frown.

"Any success identifying the others?" he asked.

"Yes, Sir. I believe so." She leaned forward and laid a photo in the center of the desk. "This is the man who crossed into Namibia with Page and with the person we believe might be Mercomes. He used an American passport under the name Manny Beg. I ran Manny Beg against all of our files and found nothing—which seems to be the pattern with these people. They disappear. We have *something* on virtually every American. Yet it seems that name has been cleared from our files and from all law enforcement and military records in the country. So I ran his picture against photo records in all three. I got a match in a group photo of a SEAL team. The members were just labeled by last name. I hadn't found it earlier because Beg is too common a word for me to have used it effectively as a single search variable."

The director slipped his ankle from his knee and leaned forward. "But you found a matching photo? And what happened to Mr.

Manny Beg?"

"He has no service record, and there is no record of him since."

The director picked up the picture. "He looks like he might be Middle Eastern or Central Asian."

"Begg, often spelled in English with two Gs, is a name you find among the mountain people of Northeast Pakistan," Amanda offered, wanting to fully disclose her research.

The director stared thoughtfully at the photo, the frown deepening for a moment, then relaxing. "Ah," he murmured. "That would explain how they disappeared so easily." He turned back to Amanda. "Another case," he explained. "I would guess that our Mr. Beg was the man who vanished into the Hunza Valley in that part of Pakistan a few years ago with a woman accomplice and a Buddhist monk. From the descriptions we've been given, I doubt the woman was your Dreu Sason. So I'd venture a guess that there is still a fourth. Probably more."

"I have only been successful in identifying the three," Amanda said. "But I will continue to search."

The director stood, and she rose with him. "You've done excellent work, Nguyen. *Excellent* work. You were clearly the right choice."

Amanda began to turn toward the door, then paused. "Might I ask, Sir, what you plan to do when we know who is part of Unit One?"

The director shook his head uncertainly. "I'm not really sure," he muttered.

45

Under the name Gabriel, she had reserved a table for five on the terrace at Strofi just south of Athens' Acropolis. The evening was perfect: 23°C with a light breeze and cloudless sky, the rich flavors of Mediterranean cooking drifting from the kitchen. She took a seat at the edge of the veranda away from the reserved table, ordered a glass of wine, a white Savatiano recommended by the waiter, and watched for the others to arrive.

On the flat hilltop to the north, floodlights turned the marble pillars of the Parthenon a creamy white. A swarm of tourists, welcoming the cooler temperatures of evening, cast tiny shadows as they moved in a steady procession across the base of the fabled temple. If it weren't for the reason for the gathering, Dreu couldn't imagine a more romantic place to be meeting Adam after nearly a month apart. But she had dressed for the reunion: floor-length black silk pants and a long-sleeved lace top, also black.

A man she judged to be Mediterranean watched her attentively from the veranda bar, finally screwing up the courage to approach. He spoke to her in English she recognized as accented by Spanish.

"I could not help but admire such a lovely woman, sitting here by herself. May I buy you a drink?"

She smiled politely and answered in the Castilian Spanish of her father. "It is most kind of you to offer. But I am waiting for my friends to arrive." She held up her glass. "And one drink is all I should have before supper."

To her relief, he bowed slightly and returned her smile. "Ah, yes," he said. "Then I will leave you to your friends. But when I saw that you seemed to be alone, I knew I would regret the rest of the evening if I did not at least attempt to make your acquaintance.

Enjoy your evening." He bowed again and returned to his perch at the bar.

She was not surprised that Tony Lee was the first to arrive. The waiter led him to the reserved table where he paused briefly before sitting and studied those gathered around the four other tables filled with evening diners. His eyes settled momentarily on Dreu but, unlike the Spaniard, showed no reaction to seeing an attractive woman seated alone. The two had never met. Like all but one of the Unit's agents, Tony had been recruited through an anonymous phone call that offered relief from a position he loved, but a circumstance he found intolerable. In Tony's case, the young Korean American had been part of a Secret Service detail assigned to the personal protection of one of the President's children he found to be ethically challenged and morally bankrupt. He had requested a transfer but had been reminded he had signed on to do what he was told.

The day Tony resigned from the service, he had been contacted by a man who introduced himself only as Gabriel. The voice on the phone offered Tony an opportunity to continue to serve his nation in a way that met the young man's personal sense of honor. Negotiations had initially been strained, then wary, and eventually completely satisfying to both Tony and the mysterious Gabriel who found the new recruit an invaluable asset for work in Asia.

Tony had just completed his second assignment, a foray into North Korea in search of two physicists who had disappeared from the South. The mission had come as a request from the CIA Director himself, based on information from US intelligence that the scientists, a man and woman, were working on nuclear development for Kim Jung-un under threat to their South Korean families.

Lee held Dreu's gaze long enough that she guessed he thought she might be more than a woman awaiting a date, then slid into a seat along the balcony railing that afforded an open view of activity across the terrace.

Dreu rose as another single woman was escorted onto the veranda, an attractive redhead with emerald eyes and light freckles she made no effort to conceal with makeup. Dreu intercepted the waiter and his charge as they neared the table.

"Hello, Britt," she said, extending a hand and nodding to the waiter that she would accompany the woman to her seat. "It's been quite some time."

The redhead paused, an amused smile creeping across her lips. "Well. Dreu Sason, if I remember correctly. Or was it Tanvi Russell?"

"Dreu Sason for this evening," Dreu assured her, taking Britt's arm and turning toward Tony who stood as they neared the table. "And this is Tony Lee. Tony has been taking care of some of our work in Asia the last few years. Tony, meet Britt Haugen, one of your Unit One colleagues."

Tony gave a quick smile and nod, shook Britt's hand, then returned his curious gaze to Dreu. "And you are . . . ?"

"Dreu Sason. I am the person who asked that you both be here this evening. Thank you for responding so quickly. Please, be seated and order something to drink. We're expecting two others who should be arriving any moment." She placed her wine glass at the rail spot opposite Tony. Britt sat beside the young Asian American, asked Dreu how she liked her wine choice and, getting an approving nod, ordered the same. Tony decided to try a Greek beer called Crazy Donkey.

"I gather you two have met," he said, directing his comment mainly to Dreu. "And you said the other two were coming together. Gabriel told me when I joined up that I would generally be working alone. Am I the only one to do solo work?"

Dreu waited while the waiter poured Britt enough wine to sniff and sip, filled her glass when she approved, and expertly eased Tony's beer into a tall glass.

"It has just been a matter of circumstances," she explained. "Britt needed some backup in a case in Europe and a couple of us stepped in. She and one of the others who is coming worked a rescue together in Pakistan. For both of your assignments so far, Tony, it has been critical that you work alone. Don't you agree?"

He cocked his head, looked with amusement at the two attractive women who might have been partners, and reluctantly nodded. "I suspect I may need to call for some help next time," he said, giving Dreu a sly wink.

"Manny must be joining us too, then," Britt guessed. As if on cue, the waiter stepped back out onto the terrace with Adam and Manny close behind. Dreu stood and beamed at the tall, angular man with his dark hair neatly trimmed since she had last seen him.

"We're all here," she said quietly. "This is all of Unit One."

Tony Lee stood awkwardly while Britt rose to pull Manny into a tight hug and Adam wrapped Dreu with both arms and kissed her with enough passion to draw applause from two surrounding tables. He kept her pulled tightly against his side as he offered his right hand to Tony.

"Anthony. So good to meet you in person. I'm Adam. You have known me as Gabriel." He turned and grinned at Britt whose tilted chin and arched brow showed his Gabriel announcement had taken her by surprise.

"Did you know this?" she demanded of Manny.

"As of about a week ago," he defended and stepped forward to introduce himself to Tony Lee.

"Please, everyone. Be seated," Adam invited and took the chair next to Dreu, leaving Manny the seat at the end of the table. "I know how unusual this all must seem—and how uncomfortable, since secrecy has been our guiding principle. But I have a great deal to share with each of you that can best be done with all of us together." He glanced around for the waiter, waved to the young man who was watching attentively from the doors onto the veranda, and picked up a menu. "First things first, though. Manny and I drove down from Kastoria this afternoon and could use a drink. Please—decide what you would like. After we have enjoyed a meal together, I will explain why we have called you all here."

"And," he added, checking that other tables on the veranda were far enough away to afford privacy, "while we eat, you are free to share with each other what you have been doing. I know it has been a lonely existence."

They settled on a selection of shared dishes: appetizers of marinated artichokes and fried squid; bowls of Greek and spinach salads; a common pot of veal stew; grilled sea bass; pork fillets stuffed with sundried tomatoes and gruyere cheese; an assorted cheese platter. Desserts were left to the individual, with the women choosing baklava and the men opting for walnut pie and ice cream.

Adam let the conversation drift in whatever direction the five wished to take it, but could feel an underlying hesitation to share secrets and a tension that told him they all knew the Unit hadn't been assembled for the first time simply to feast on Greek cuisine with a breathtaking, twilight view of the Acropolis. When everyone had been served either coffee, cappuccino, or an after-dinner ouzo, he placed his cup on the table, sat back with hands in lap, and found that he immediately had the attention of four sets of eyes.

"This is, of course, an unprecedented gathering," he began, pausing to look at each of his colleagues. "Three of us were recruited into Unit One by its founder, a carryover from the old OSS days of the CIA we knew as Fisher. I know it was explained to each of you when you signed on that the Unit was created when the Agency came to believe that it was receiving too much public scrutiny, the kind of open examination that made it difficult to impossible to handle some of the most sensitive challenges facing our nation, or some that were internal and off limits. Our job was to clean up messes or handle assignments the CIA felt were too politically charged."

He scanned his listeners who remained silent, but nodded their understanding.

"Dreu and I had the good fortune to work for a number of years with the woman who was selected from day one to be Fisher's colleague, companion, confidant, and computer expert. Her name was Anita. You may have spoken to her if you ever contacted the center when I—or Fisher before my time—wasn't available." Adam smiled and gave Dreu a nostalgic glance. "You would remember her, I'm sure, because you would have thought you were talking to Sofia Vergara. Rich Spanish accent. Anyway, after Fisher's death, she stayed with us until her own. At least once a week she reminded us that the Unit had two guiding principles: do the right things for the country, not necessarily for the Agency; and remain completely independent and anonymous. After the CIA director who worked with Fisher to create the Unit left office, no director since has known who Fisher was or where he was located. They all wanted it that way. Maximum deniability. And we have continued to maintain that separation. Aside from assignments that required two agents—or, in at least one case, three—you haven't even known about each other. All for our protection and yours."

Another quick scan of the troubled faces around the table told Adam they were getting a pretty clear sense where this was going. He spared them further suspense.

"For some reason, that has all changed with this director. I guess we make him uneasy. We have learned that he has tasked a cyber-operations specialist internally to learn all she can about the Unit, including who and where we are. She is very talented, and she now knows Dreu and I are part of the team, and you, Manny."

The Middle East specialist nodded grimly. "I can see how that could happen," he admitted. "I asked not to change my name and used it on my passport on this Africa assignment."

Adam shrugged. "Nothing would have tied you to us if they hadn't been tracking me," he said. "And we're not here to accuse anyone. Each of you has exceeded our expectations in everything you have done. But three of us have been outed, and I suspect you will be next, Tony." He looked across the table at Britt. "You, Miss Haugen, will be harder to find. Janet McIntire died in that explosion in England, and I think we did a pretty thorough job of getting rid of her old records. But as I said, this woman is good."

"Has it always been the director who has handed down assignments?" Tony asked, picking up a remaining bread stick and twirling it slowly between his fingers.

Adam's grin was humorless. "Not always. And I suspect you put your finger on part of the man's nervousness. Fisher was initially given latitude to identify challenges he thought the Unit should pursue and make independent judgments. We've kept that as part of our mission. On at least two occasions, we've found ourselves at cross-purposes with the Agency. One of them, Manny and I just came from. And it has been an especially troubling one." He gave the group a quick summary of his effort to find and rescue Nick Page and the killing of the former operative in Windhoek. "And that," he concluded, "is why I asked Dreu to bring you all together here. I won't risk having that happen to one of us."

"Do you know it was an Agency hit?" Britt asked.

"No. In fact, some of the CIA people trying to follow us in Africa seemed genuinely surprised."

"But. . ." she prompted.

"But we don't know that it wasn't. And to be perfectly honest, if there is a group like us that cleans up messes the government has created—one that only the director knows about—who's to say there isn't another team that takes care of individuals who might know too much or be an embarrassment? And let's see—three of us here know all about Marburg and the attempt by our government to acquire biological weapons in violation of the 1972 accords. Three of us, and not all the same people, know that a disaffected CIA agent was gunned down a few days ago in Namibia. And since the Agency doesn't know who's on our team and how we operate, they probably assume all of us know everything. To quote one of our former Secretaries of Defense, it's the 'unknown unknowns' that are making me uneasy."

The table sat in silence, each agent soaking in what the man who handed out assignments that could potentially draw the Agency's ire had just said.

"So," Manny said finally, "what are you feeling we need to do?"

Adam reached beside him and squeezed the hands that fidgeted nervously in Dreu's lap, then stared off thoughtfully across the stretch of dimly lit city at the skeleton of the temple that glowed in bright relief against the night sky.

"Do any of you know what a boma is?" he asked, his gaze still on the ruin. Without looking about for a response, he explained.

"Before Manny picked us up two days ago," he murmured, softly enough that the four had to lean attentively toward him, "Nick and I were spending our nights in what the Africans call a boma—a sheltering ring of thorny branches cut from an acacia tree. Nick told me one night that he found a certain comfort inside the circle, knowing the things he feared—the threats that were after him—were kept at bay." He looked again at his companions, tightening his hand around Dreu's.

"But the thing I realized as we talked that evening," he continued, "was that when you are in the boma, you are also trapped. If something gets in, you have nowhere to go. You could fight for your life, or try to tear your way through the barbs and spears you thought were protecting you." He smiled sadly across at Britt. "And we are trapped in the kind of life that destroyed Nick. No friends. No family. No one to love or be loved by." He leaned over and kissed his partner's cheek and she nuzzled against his shoulder.

"I've been fortunate, and selfish, to have Dreu. I know that Britt has someone she loves very much, but has had to keep at arm's length. But we've lived this way long enough. And someone is gradually tearing the limbs away from our boma. So tonight," he said firmly, "I am disbanding Unit One. As of this moment, you are all free to do whatever you feel inspired to do. I am asking, of course, that this part of your life remain secret. Just tell people you worked for a government agency that required an oath of secrecy, and leave it at that." Another more abrupt squeeze to Dreu's hands let her know it was her time to step in.

"But we aren't going to just leave you out in the cold and penniless," she added with a resigned smile. "At least Britt is aware that we intercepted the payment from the top bidder for the Marburg virus and socked it away in a very secure place. Since then, it has been gaining interest. After Adam contacted me about this decision, I had it divided into five individual accounts, each with your own personal number. Though I set them up, I haven't kept a record of the numbers, so don't lose them." She drew three envelopes from her clutch and handed one to Britt, Tony, and Manny. "This should keep you for a year or two."

Britt slipped a finger beneath the flap, slid it through the top of the envelope, drew out the single slip of paper, then looked up at the two across from her, swallowing her surprise. Manny had ripped the end from his and opened the page.

"Holy shit!" The exclamation turned the heads of English speakers at other tables. "Sorry," he said more softly, then added in a whisper, "Fifty million dollars?"

"The Marburg auction ended at $250 million," Dreu said. "We gave a few million to Fisher's Norwegian friend who alerted us to the deal, but we've earned that back ten times over. This is a five-way split, with some left in the account, should we ever need to revive it."

"And this doesn't belong to anyone else?" Tony asked.

"We weren't positive who the buyer was," Adam explained. "But it was some nation or terrorist group with no good intentions. You will make better use of the money."

"And you didn't need to use some of this to fund operations?" he asked.

"Ironically," Adam said with a grim chuckle, "the CIA has included us in its black ops budget for sixty years. An appropriation is sent to an account each budget year, and Dreu moves it into an operational fund only we can access. It will be much harder for the Agency to find than identifying the five of us. We've never spent it all, and it is now pretty sizable. We plan to leave it for now—just in case."

"In case of a new director?" Britt suggested. "A more accepting attitude about arm's length?"

Adam shrugged. "Once it's known who we are—by anyone—it will be difficult to put the genie back in the bottle. To become unknown again. But I've learned to never say never." He signaled the waiter and ordered five glasses of ouzo.

"And what do you two plan to do?" Britt asked with a curious smile.

Adam lifted Dreu's hands to his lips as the waiter passed around the drinks.

"I have a friend who needs to be properly buried," he said, raising his glass, "and a little score to settle. Then we plan to become part of the Unknowns." He cast an eye about the table. "But here is to four of the finest people I could ever have dreamed of working with. And here is to Unit One."

46

Marshall Pollard sat stiffly in front of the director's desk with the formality of a man who was old-school CIA. Beside him, Justin Turnley was more relaxed, leaning loosely on one elbow on an arm of his chair.

"We traced our way back through Nick Page's movements to see who was asking about him or showing up where he did," Pollard reported. "In addition to this Robert Solomon, who was something of a latecomer, we discovered that a Severu Messina appears to have been tracking him since shortly after Page left Syria. We assume this is the same Severu Messina who was involved in the Syrian prisoner swap and guess there was bad blood between them. Probably because of Messina's capture and torture. Our assessment is that it was Messina who got to Page in Windhoek."

The director sat with fingers steepled thoughtfully beneath his chin. "And what has happened to Messina?" he asked.

Turnley answered for the Africa team. "All of our people across Southern Africa are looking for him, but he has disappeared. We trained the man well."

The director thought for another moment, then stood suddenly. "Thank you, gentlemen. And good work on the Page problem. Unfortunate ending, but great work on your parts. I hope you both plan to take a few extra days in Washington before returning to station." He didn't offer to shake hands, and the station chiefs gave a quick nod and left the office.

The director dropped heavily back into his chair. Severu Messina was becoming a liability—potentially a greater one than Page had ever been. He had used Messina a few times for assignments like this. The man was in a constant rage and appeared to have lost all traces of a moral compass. But if Messina had taken down Nick Page, the director hadn't sanctioned the hit. He couldn't afford to have a rogue killer on the loose with no conscience. He had worried about the Unit 1 team becoming too independent, but they hadn't done anything like this. It might be time to use his newfound information about the Unit as leverage to get them to solve this new problem for him.

It looked like the North Korean hostage mess he had asked Gabriel to assist with had been resolved. And as well as he could have hoped. The scientists had both been secreted out of the North and reunited with their families under FBI protection in California. But what the hell was going on in Venezuela with the warehouses full of bleached currency the Unit people suspected was a massive counterfeiting scheme to produce passable US bills? The director had given Gabriel the green light to investigate, then hadn't heard a thing. It was past time for a follow-up and for him to let this Gabriel know things weren't going to operate as they had in the past.

He entered a password into his computer, waited for the validation device he carried in his shirt pocket to buzz with the second-tier security code, then entered the file in which he kept his director-only contact numbers. From the back of his center desk drawer, he drew out a dedicated phone, began to enter the Unit's number, then paused. After a moment's consideration, he placed the phone on the desk top and called down to Cyber Operations.

"Could you send Officer Nguyen up to see me?" he asked, and waited until Amanda was ushered into the office and sat rigidly in the chair Officer Pollard had just occupied.

47

Mt. Etna's irritability had grown until now, in the fading light of evening, a red glow capped the top of the crater. The Sicilian stepped onto his veranda, lifted the umbrella from its support in the center of the deck table, and shook off the coating of ash that had accumulated during his absence. Someday, he thought, the mountain was going to explode again and all life on the island would be extinguished. Perhaps it would be tomorrow. Or tonight while he slept.

Though he doubted it would be tonight, if the mountain goddess should decide to take him in his sleep, he would prefer that he not be alone. He pulled out his cell and dialed his travel agent.

"Sylvie, I am back in town," he announced when he heard the familiar voice. "I thought perhaps you could join me at *Da Lorenzo* for supper. I haven't had a good Italian meal for a week. And then perhaps we could come back to my place for drinks."

"So. You are home again." Her tone was cool—and suspicious. "Where was it this time, Sev? Angola? You have interesting travel habits for a merchant in nuts and olive oil who only seems to work when he is suddenly called away to one troubled place or another. Are the Angolans needing more olive oil? Or is it chestnuts?"

"Sylvie," he muttered, "we have been over this before. I am just a middleman. All my work arrangements can be made from home. I travel simply to finalize agreements. Can't we just have a nice meal together without you worrying about where my business takes me?"

"And a nice night together afterward, I would guess," she said acidly. "I am through with all that, Severu. You seem to want my company only when the spirit moves you—or when you want a night of sex. And if you truly did want more, I have come to realize there is a very good chance you may not come back from one of these *business* trips. I am sorry, Sev. I will continue to happily send you wherever you wish to go, but I will not be your convenient dinner and bed companion when it suits you."

The phone went dead against Sev's ear. He held it there for a moment, then lowered it onto the table. If Etna decided to take him tonight, it appeared that he would be alone.

48

"I need to check in with our colleagues in Unit One—wherever they may be," the director told Amanda with a confiding smile. "I thought I should get an update before I let them know that our former degree of separation is no longer acceptable. Do you have any new information for me?"

"I believe my search of disaffected government security personnel may have identified another team member," she admitted hesitantly. "But I am yet to confirm him. He has a very common Korean name, and there are tens of thousands of men with the same name I need to eliminate before being certain this man disappeared."

"Not critical," the director assured her. "We have what we need. And I thought, as the only other internal person who knows about the Unit, you might appreciate being party to our first action to bring them a little more closely into the fold. And I might need to check a fact or two with you during the conversation. I'll be asking for a report on an action we agreed to pursue in Venezuela, and there is another little matter I need their help with."

"What if they ask about me?" she wondered. "They believe they know who I am."

"Who you are is none of their concern," he assured her and again picked up the phone. With great deliberation, he entered the Unit 1 number, hit *Send*, and switched the device to speaker.

The phone buzzed only once, then clicked at the other end. Before the director could speak, a silky-smooth female voice announced, "The number you have reached is no longer in service and there is no new number. The party that used to be at this number existed only as long as it didn't exist. And I might remind you, should we start feeling pursued, *all* of us know more than you would want to be made public. If you have some new mess that needs to be cleared up, good luck. It is all yours. Goodbye."

"*What the hell?*" the director spouted, pushing from his chair and turning away from her.

Across the desk, Amanda Nguyen kept her eyes on the hands folded in her lap. "Do you need me for anything else?" she asked respectfully.

"No . . . no. Not now. I'll call if I need you."

She stood and left the office with the director still muttering curses at his neatly arranged bookcase.

Back in her cubicle, the cyber-operations officer sat in silence for a long moment, staring at the monitor through which she had sparred with the fabled Dreu Sason. Then she smiled a faint, very personal smile, tapped her computer back to life, accessed the site where they had exchanged messages, and typed:

I will miss you, Dreu Sason—and Tom, and Manny, and Tony Lee, and the yet-to-be-identified red-haired woman. And so will our country. You know how to reach me.

Author's Notes

With each of the Unit 1 thrillers, in addition to weaving a story I hope will entertain and captivate my readers, my goal is for them to come away from the book with a better understanding of the part of the world in which the book is set: in this case, Southern Africa.

Kabwe in Zambia, in addition to remaining seriously polluted by colonial mining during the late 19th and early 20th centuries, is indeed the sight of the discovery of Homo heidelbergensis, the Rhodesia Man, or the Broken Hill man. Some scientists believe the skull, discovered by a Swiss miner in the Broken Hill Mine in 1921, represents a transitional stage between early Homo erectus, Neanderthals, and modern humans. In 2020, sophisticated dating techniques placed the age of the skull at between 274,000 and 324,000 years old.

Shortly after its discovery, the mining company sent the skull to the British National Museum, where it now remains, though efforts are underway to get it returned to Zambia. Kabwe is still courageously working to reclaim land left barren by this mining activity, but faces a long, uphill battle.

The Angolan civil war (1975-2002) has left that country in a similar state of devastation. Many of its endemic species, including the rare Giant Angolan or Giant Sable Antelope, are on the brink of extinction as a result of nearly three decades of internal fighting. Hunting of the Giant Sable Antelope is now strictly forbidden and what few remain are in several national parks in the eastern part of Angola. The countryside west of the road that connects Kuito to Namibia remains densely covered with landmines.

At the risk of becoming overly political, I feel the need to comment on the Syrian civil war. I had the unusual opportunity of spending part of the summer of 2007 in Syria with a group that was studying religious pluralism in "secular" Muslim countries. As a result of extraordinary planning by the Syrian co-director of this Fulbright Fellowship, we were able to meet with a number of senior government ministers, the Grand Mufti of Syria (the leader of the majority of Syrian Muslims); the Patriarch of the Syrian Christian Church; and a small Jewish congregation that met in an ancient synagogue in Damascus. We traveled widely in the country, spoke freely with citizens in most of the major cities, and were guided by a Syrian Christian whose family had been displaced from the Golan Heights during the 1967 Arab-Israeli Conflict. Everywhere we went, the feeling among the citizenry was that, as much as the people had disliked Hafez al-Assad, they saw great hope in the leadership of his son, Bashar al-Assad. The co-director I mentioned was the daughter of a man who had been imprisoned for twelve years by the senior Assad. Yet even her family saw new and positive efforts to reform by the son. Admittedly, the army had considerable influence on Bashar al-Assad and kept a tight rein on him. But generally, the future looked promising.

When the teens in Syria's southern city of Daraa committed their acts of vandalism in 2011, that army did overreact in a brutal, violent way. But there was a strong belief that, given immediate and broad-based pressure by the US and other nations, the government might back off and work to restore order through negotiations. The move by the US and Western powers was instead to support the uprising, hoping to unseat Assad. We are now painfully familiar with the result. (The Homsi assassination presented in this book is my fictional creation.)

I add this postscript to highlight the complexities and fragile nature of international politics and to show how ill-considered decisions can have lengthy and far-reaching negative consequences. I am admittedly pretty hard on the CIA in this book while, in reality, I have great respect for the agency and its work. Fortunately, for a writer who depends on policy missteps for plot ideas, there always seems to be a fertile list.

RING OF THORNS

OTHER BOOKS BY ALLEN KENT

<u>Unit 1 International Thrillers</u>

The Shield of Darius
The Weavers of Meanchey
The Wager
The Marburg Mutation
Straits of the Between

<u>The Whitlock Series (Historical fiction)</u>

River of Light and Shadow
Wild Whistling Blackbirds
Suzanna's Song

<u>The Colby Tate Mysteries</u>

Murder One
Eye for an Eye

<u>Mystery/Thrillers</u>

Backwater
Guardians of the Second Son

<u>Young Adult</u>

Switch

Made in the USA
Monee, IL
22 March 2021